I0762043

CURSE OF THE TROLL

A RETELLING OF EAST OF THE SUN, WEST OF THE MOON

EMMA HAMM

Copyright © 2019 by Emma Hamm

All rights reserved.

No part of this book may be reproduced in any form or by any electronic or mechanical means, including information storage and retrieval systems, without written permission from the author, except for the use of brief quotations in a book review.

❀ Created with Vellum

This is for you.

PROLOGUE

Once upon a time, in a faraway land, a faerie princess fell in love with a dwarf. He wasn't like other men. His beard was long, his eyes dark, and he barely came up to her shoulder. But he was kind, and he understood her need for war.

But the dwarf was cursed. He couldn't love her as long as the Troll Queen laid claim to his body.

She lived with him as the curse grew stronger. Every day, he hated his monstrous form all the more. Every night, he lamented his inability to be beside her.

The faerie princess didn't have it in her to tell him she couldn't be with him. Not as a normal woman. There was no heart in her chest, only a gaping hole, rendered there by so many men who had not believed in her. Men who had hurt her, maimed her, made it impossible for her to know how to love.

The dwarf wasn't afraid. He loved her more than enough for the both of them, he said, but in that moment, the Troll Queen stole him away.

East of the sun, the princess had to travel. West of the moon, she had to go. A slice of the world hidden between sunlight and darkness. All the way to the troll kingdom, she journeyed to save him.

When the faerie princess made it, she realized it wouldn't be as easy as she thought. The trolls were crafty. They wanted a price for his hand, and it was a price she didn't know how to pay.

A golden apple, so pretty it reflected the sunlight deep within it, was the only thing she could offer. The faerie princess gave the Troll Queen this gift, and in return, asked to see the dwarf. When the troll agreed, she found the dwarf asleep in his cell.

The next time, the princess brought with her a golden necklace, and the inset emerald gemstones caught the eye of the Troll Queen, who snatched the necklace immediately.

This time, the dwarf remained awake through the poison just enough to tell her to fight for him.

And so she did.

The faerie princess gave the troll a sword and told it to fight. To prove she was worthy of this dwarf's love when the princess barely felt worthy herself. They battled as only legendary warriors could.

When she won, breathing hard and slick with sweat, she reached out for the dwarf.

"I love you," he said.

"I cannot love you back," she replied. "My heart is gone, and I don't know where to search for it."

The dwarf placed his hand on her chest and, suddenly, a heart grew where there had not been one before. "I've had it the whole time," he said. "Now, I can give it back to you.

1

Elva slashed at the straw man in front of her. Over and over, she hacked with her sword until there were tufts of yellow sticking out from its torso in all directions. She had to train, had to be ready for the next time when someone needed her blade. Or when she had to protect herself.

The last thought stuck in her mind. *Protect herself. Be someone who knew how to stand up to another person and say no.*

Sweat dripped from her forehead into her eyes. The sting reminded her she was training for a reason. She didn't want anyone to feel the pain that she had felt in her life. No other woman or man should be forced to marry someone they didn't want to marry.

But she hadn't really been forced, had she?

Memories slipped through her rigid control of a night with a man who had made her smile. He'd tucked a strand of her silvery hair behind her ear and chuckled at a joke she couldn't remember. He had been beautiful in the moonlight, keeping her gaze and attention from anyone who might have loved her more.

Her husband, ex-husband now, she reminded herself, had once been a good man. Fionn had loved her more than the sun in the sky and had tried so hard to make her happy. But the King of the Seelie Fae had never wanted her to be his queen. He had told her he wanted to save her from the struggles of living in the palace with eyes watching her every step. She would be his concubine, his pretty little kept thing, and they'd be happy together.

Until they hadn't been.

Happiness had given way to arguments, to resentment, and then she'd drifted away from him. His voice whispered in her ear even now.

The swish of the blade became his musical voice. "Why can't you love me like you used to? We were perfect together. Why can't you make yourself feel that again?"

Because they'd both changed into someone they hadn't been. Because he'd found himself addicted to opium and then convinced her to try it as well. Elva hadn't recognized herself around him. How could she when the world had turned into nothing more than a hazy version of itself?

She whirled, lifting the deadly blade above her head and striking it down. His violet eyes stared back at her, reflected in the silver metal.

With a snarl, she twisted on her heel. She shifted her weight, holding the blade higher and drawing it across the throat of the straw man. The blade was sharpened to a perfect point. It sliced through the material wrapped around the straw with ease.

For a moment, the straw man's head remained where it was. There were no eyes to stare back at her, but she still saw the man who had made her believe he was something more than just a spoiled brat. Something more than just a prince who wanted another pretty bauble to put on his shelf and stare at.

She saw the King of the Seelie Fae, who was now banished to the mortal realm, removed from his throne but just as beautiful as he'd been when she had married him. She saw Fionn, and she didn't know how to see anything else.

Slowly, the head of the straw man tilted to the side, then fell onto the ground. The soft hush of straw hitting dirt cleared her mind. Blade still lifted, she stared through the hole revealed by her movements.

Elva lived on the Isle of Skye with the rest of the women who were training to be warriors. Each had their own reason for being here. Some wanted to fulfil their dead brother's promises to family. Some wanted revenge on people who had hurt them. Others had nowhere else to go and thus had turned to war and violence.

Whatever reason brought them here, Scáthach took them in. She was the most decorated warrior ever known to mankind. She'd trained Cú Chulainn himself.

The training grounds were little more than a field outside the keep where Scáthach lived. Rows upon rows of tents lined the fields. Those who were training weren't permitted to sleep within the keep. Sleeping on the hard ground would prepare them for their difficult lives ahead. Elva preferred it anyway. She didn't want someone sneaking into her room at night. Here, she could control every bit of her life.

Visitors to the Isle of Skye were ignored. If they drew a blade, they were all confident it wouldn't leave its sheath before at least three warrior women destroyed the person who attempted to draw it.

Now, all of her fellow warriors were lined up on the road. Never had she seen the warrior women stop in their training for someone. Each woman held a hand on the hilt of their blades, staring at the newcomer with mistrust and...hatred? Elva had never seen so much hatred on their faces before.

She remained where she was, sword lifted above her head, and watched as the most miraculous thing she'd ever seen strode toward her.

A bear.

Larger than any other bear, this was more than just an animal, but a monstrous beast. His shoulder was taller than her, taller even than the biggest woman here in the training camp. Brown fur covered his body and dark, black eyes watched the women with an equal amount of mistrust.

It had to be a male. She'd never seen a bear grow to be so large, certainly not in these parts. Elva hadn't even heard of bears on the Isle of Skye.

Great paws slapped at the ground. He didn't speak, but it had to be something more than just an animal. A beast of the wild would have attacked someone by now. This one seemed to know where he was going. He walked with a confidence that belayed his intelligence.

Elva stood frozen where she was, not moving even when he stared directly into her eyes. Those eyes had so much emotion in them that it made her head spin. Hunger lurked in the shadows of that gaze, but something sad as well. Something that made her own soul turn away in fear.

Elva didn't want to see something of herself in this creature. He couldn't be anything she could help, no cursed man or creature who needed her involvement. She'd dedicated her entire life to being a warrior, a woman who protected those who needed her, not to find her attention captured by a beast.

She forced herself to turn away from him.

The bear walked by her, the ground shaking under his great weight as he passed. Claws scraped the ground so close to her foot, the gravel skittered. And then he was gone.

Her gaze lifted to follow his path. Would he look back?

Did she want him to?

Another of the warrior women, Deirdre, whose story was worse than Elva's, stepped up to her side. "That's the Beast of Fuar Bheinn."

"Who?" Elva had never heard of such a creature. She'd come from the Seelie court in Ireland and hadn't spent much time exploring the faerie realm of Scotland. There was much here she still didn't know.

"Fuar Bheinn, the cold mountain. It's always covered in snow, even in the greatest warmth of the summer. Ice never melts there, and the cold blasts of air will freeze even the greatest warrior's hearts."

Elva snorted. "Seems like a myth more than a reality."

"I've been there before." Deirdre's fingers twisted together as she shifted restlessly with nerves. "Naoise and his brothers thought we could run through the mountains to get away from the man I was promised to marry. We had to come back down. The storms there are treacherous, but it wasn't the snow or the ice that sent us running."

"What did?" Elva already knew what the woman was going to say. It made her turn her gaze back toward the keep. The bear had nearly reached the gates that already stood open, awaiting his arrival.

"The screams," Deirdre replied. "The wind carries them until it's all you can hear. Something on that mountain is in great pain."

"Why didn't you try to help it?"

"Sometimes the screams weren't from pain. Sometimes they were from rage, and then there were more voices that joined them." Deirdre shivered. "I wouldn't go back to that place if someone paid me to do so. There's more there than just a beast on a mountain."

As Deirdre strode away, Elva continued to stare back at the keep. Who was that beast? And what did he want here, of all places?

She could only hope Scáthach sent him on his way as quickly as he'd arrived. No one here wanted to help him. This was a tribe of women who had been scorned by men one too many times. They didn't save those who had put themselves in harm's way.

Of course, her dearest of friends would tell her that was dangerous thinking. Bran wanted to see her happy, or at least happier than she was right now. Considering he was the man she had *wanted* to marry originally, and the man who was now married to her sister, Elva realized she should probably listen to him.

After all, he was an Unseelie king and keeper of the largest army known to faerie kind. He'd done more in his first few years as king than most would ever do in their lifetime. If he was taking the time to speak, then it was probably something important.

But she never listened to him, though. Even when they were just children in fields of golden wheat, playing at being in love, she'd always done the opposite of what he wanted her to do. The mere idea of someone telling her how to be or act had made her rebel immediately.

Until, of course, she'd married. Then she'd done whatever her husband had wanted. She'd been whoever he wanted.

Look at where that had gotten her.

She tried so hard not to remember that time, but the memories always threatened to swallow her whole. They rose in her mind, bubbling like a witch's brew and popping at the worst moments.

One of them arose in her mind now, filling her with the memory of the sweet scent of licorice and the spice of pepper. Fionn had always smelled like candy and something that burned.

Elva felt his finger stroke down her arm, the slow glide so smooth it was clear he'd never worked a day in her life. He had always marveled at her beauty, at the way her flesh was nearly hairless, so much so that it sometimes made her sick to her stomach. He hadn't ever seen her as anything more than a bauble, a toy he could take out when he wanted. Every time he complimented her looks, she had been reminded of how little he loved *her*.

He had loved her because she was beautiful, not for who she was.

But she couldn't blame him entirely. She had married him because she wanted to be a queen. Because her mother had pushed her to be something she wasn't.

"Be beautiful," her mother used to say. "Beauty gets you more places in this life than intelligence or brute strength, Elva. You're choosing now to either work the rest of your life or have someone else do the work for you. Wouldn't you rather have pretty things?"

At the time, that had sounded perfect. Never having to worry about lighting the braziers or getting her own food? That was a life of luxury.

Now, she realized, it was so far from what she wanted. Elva wanted to work for what she earned, not be given something because another person thought she might give them something in return.

She was done bartering with her body. Now, she was the beast that roamed the forest, making deals. Not the little girl wandering through the shadows, hoping to avoid creatures that might eat her alive.

Sliding her sword back into its sheath, she stared up at the keep and prayed something wasn't about to change. That bear had made her stomach churn.

And Elva had learned to always trust her gut.

2

He carefully placed one paw in front of the other, trying his best to look less intimidating. The last thing he needed was one of these warriors to assume he was here to attack their stronghold. He could destroy them all if he wanted.

But he didn't.

Donnacha chuffed out a breath as one of the warrior women stepped a little too close for comfort. Her eyes flicked side-to-side, planning out her next move if he stepped a foot out of line. He would have done the same thing if something like him had stepped into his home.

Anyone with a good head on their shoulders would assume a massive bear wasn't here for something good. He was either here to destroy them, their mistress, or their home. What other possibilities were there?

They'd never guess why he was really here. Donnacha was certain of that. The curse that had turned him into a beast was an ancient spell known only by a few. Thus, only a few would know how to break the curse.

He hadn't known how to break it himself until the blasted woman who had cursed him in the first place had arrived in his castle. She'd only told him the single loophole because she knew he'd never be able to break the curse. Still, he had to at least try.

Scáthach and her women were the only creatures brave enough to try. He had to beg on hands and knees for them to help him, even though he knew it was going to be a long shot that this would work.

He stepped beyond the front gates, entering the training grounds. He cast a glance across the women here. They were all strong creatures. They would have made his ancestors proud.

Long ago, Donnacha had been a dwarf. One of the royal line, he was destined to be a duke who would have taken care of his people with a discerning eye and a kindness passed down from his father. Strange how those were the first two qualities he'd lost to the curse.

Now, he looked at these women and wondered how long it would take him to swipe a paw and barrel them all down. They would fall. Everyone always fell when they tried to attack him. But he wouldn't feel good about destroying these women.

As he walked farther into the training grounds, his gaze caught with that of a rather fierce creature. Her blond hair shone in the sunlight, nearly silver and metallic. Those blue eyes stared at him with so much hatred in their depths, he wondered if they had known each other in a previous life. He didn't remember ever dealing with the Seelie Fae, and she had to be Seelie.

She watched him move, the sword lifted above her head, never wavering despite its weight. Perhaps she would be the one to destroy him after all.

Here he had been, thinking these women couldn't do a single thing to him, and one already had changed his mind. Her gaze was sharp, her body honed for battle, and she looked like she would stop at nothing.

Donnacha had learned a long time ago that the best warriors were the ones willing to give up their own lives in pursuit of their orders. She most certainly was that kind of warrior.

Who was this woman with the flint and steel eyes?

He couldn't get distracted. He had a curse to break, and no matter what others might think, he didn't want to be stuck in this form forever.

Donnacha huffed out a breath and continued toward Scáthach's keep. She would have to welcome him, no matter how much she hated him. The long journey to her doors was enough to allow him a few days of rest. Although she would probably only offer him a few hours respite before she tossed him from her doorstep.

They'd left the doors to the keep open for him. Considerate, since he couldn't grip door knobs with his paws.

He padded into the keep and tried to keep the thunderous sound of his breathing quieter. He'd learned a long time ago the huffing breaths of the bear sounded very much like he was growling, especially when echoing inside a stone building. The women were already here for a reason. They had suffered more than most of their sex, or perhaps, the same amount but were the brave ones who had run. Either way, they didn't deserve to be intimidated by a creature who had no right to ask for help.

The interior of the keep was the same as he remembered from years ago. When he had been nothing more than a boy, he'd come here with his father's men. Those were the days when Scáthach had allowed males into her home willingly. Before she had been betrayed by the man who she trusted most.

Three long tables arrowed toward the main table set horizontal at the front. Stag heads were mounted around the room, with bear and wolf pelts stretched out on the ceiling. Scáthach was a renowned huntress. It didn't escape his notice that her eyes lit up the moment she saw him.

The woman of the hour sat at the head table, feet crossed at the ankle and arms crossed behind her head. She said nothing as he approached carefully, avoiding the tables so he didn't knock anything to the floor.

When he was close, she finally spoke. "Donnacha of Clan Fuar Bheinn. I hadn't thought to see you in my keep."

His lips were not a human's, so his words were lisped. His tongue stuck in his mouth. It didn't want to form around the human sounds, but he made them. Donnacha had worked for years to be able to speak in this form. It was a badge of pride that he could still communicate with those who knew him. "A dangerous choice, I've been told."

"Indeed." Scáthach looked him up and down.

In her younger years, she had been a beautiful woman. Tangled blond hair, eyes the color of grass, and a body hardened by life. Now, he saw the telltale signs of age. Wrinkles marred her forehead and winged out from her eyes. Strong muscles were now showing signs of deterioration. Gray hair flecked the golden locks. And yet, she was still a beautiful woman. Far more beautiful than he'd thought she would age to be.

Donnacha bowed, lowering his great head and touching his chin to the ground. "I wouldn't have come if circumstances weren't dire."

"I cannot imagine what the fabled beast of cold mountain could ask of me." Scáthach unlaced her fingers behind her head and leveled him with a glare. "But it's rude to speak of such things without first feasting."

"You wish me to break bread with you?"

"I wish for entertainment." The feral grin on her face was a clear sign she wanted to embarrass him.

Fine. If she wanted to see him bend a knee and show just how bad the curse had gotten, then so be it. He needed her help and would pay any price she requested.

Donnacha folded his great, furred body by the nearest table. He wouldn't sit in a chair—his weight would only snap the delicate wood like a twig—but he could at least pretend to be human. Seated at the end of the table, he tilted his head and eyed the relaxed huntress. "Now what?" he asked, his voice gruff.

"Now we eat," Scáthach replied.

She really wanted a show then. A few of her women started to bring in food. A veritable feast with a whole roasted pig, vegetables, and all manner of sweets. He hadn't expected food, but perhaps he'd arrived at the right time.

Donnacha watched as they laid the food out in front of him. "Were you planning on a large dinner tonight?"

"A celebration," she replied.

"For what?"

"Of life. We enjoy our time on this earth while we have it, Donnacha. Perhaps you have forgotten the festivals of your clan."

One of the warrior women poured him a glass of ale. He stared at the tankard, remembering quite clearly the way his clan had enjoyed themselves. The festivals had lasted for days. The ale had flowed through the mugs so quickly they'd had to find more barrels, usually in the cellars of the stingiest dwarves.

He couldn't drink the ale anymore. His bear stomach rebelled, violently throwing up whatever he ate or drank that was consumed by humans.

Donnacha growled low his throat. "What do you want from me, Scáthach?"

She leaned forward, placing her elbows on the table in front of her. "I want to see how the fabled dwarven warrior eats now. Are you like an animal, Donnacha? Do you feast with claws and teeth?"

Of course, he did. In the privacy of his own home, he did what he must to stay alive. He'd tried desperately to be human in the first few years of this form, but utensils didn't fit in his paws. He had to use his claws to eat most things. He couldn't hold onto bread like a man. His paws weren't fingers.

He lifted the corner of his lip in disgust as he stared at the roasted pig in front of him. "Is this what you want then? To watch a bear eat in front of you?"

"I want to know just how bad the curse has gotten. I want to see for myself that you are turning into nothing more than an animal."

Donnacha snarled then, baring his teeth in an angry sound and placing his paws firmly on the table. "I'm more than an animal."

"Prove it then. Feast like a human."

"I cannot."

"Then are you really more than an animal? You used to be a dwarf. You remember how to use a fork and knife, don't you?"

"I do."

She leaned back in her chair, the picture of relaxation, but he saw the calculating look in her eye. "Then you think being human is a state of mind."

"It's a state of being."

"Your being is clearly not human." Scáthach gestured at his furred form. "What would you call yourself then?"

"Cursed."

"Tell me of your curse. Who did this to you?"

The words immediately froze on Donnacha's tongue. He couldn't tell anyone about the curse. He couldn't say anything more than he was cursed, or his entire body would freeze up. Thus, he could only stare at Scáthach in anger.

"How do we break this curse of yours?"

Again, he said nothing.

"How long are you to be cursed?"

Forever, he wanted to tell her. There was only one thing that could break this curse, and that was if someone could see through the mask of fur and claws long enough to stay with him for a year and a day. That was all he needed, a woman who would remain true for that long, despite what he looked like.

He didn't really know the logistics of it. The Troll Queen who had cursed him had set the rules, and those rules were loose at best and could be manipulated. She wasn't exactly the brightest woman in the world.

Donnacha shook his head. "I grow tired of these games, Scáthach."

"So do I. And yet, you are the one who showed up in my keep, uninvited. You know how I feel about men arriving without my permission."

Did he ever. From what he'd heard, Scáthach particularly enjoyed tearing men apart from the testicles up. He sniffed loudly and cleared his throat. "Yes, I heard the last one who arrived here and attempted to harm your trainees ended up being set on fire."

"And where did I set him on fire?"

"Uh..." Donnacha tried hard not to laugh as he said the words. "I believe the rumor said it was the most precious jewels of his family."

"There's a lot on you that's far more flammable than that man, I'll tell you that, Donnacha. So let's get right to the bottom of it so I can invite all my dear trainees in so we might celebrate living another year on the Isle of Skye. Just what do you want?"

That was why she'd everything set up while he was sitting in front of her. If she hadn't, then they wouldn't have gotten everything done in time for the feast. Now, she was going to be rushing him out of her keep, ready to entertain as though he had never been there.

Smart, he'd give her that. It was a ruse that had kept her women working and him sitting right in the middle of all that movement without a single peep.

"I need one of your women," he said softly. No matter what words he said, they were going to come out wrong. He'd already known that. Donnacha had spent most of the trip trying to figure out the best way to ask her. "I can't tell you why. I need the one whose hair is like sunlight, who could kill a bear, and who is renowned throughout the land as the prettiest fighter in the courts."

He'd asked the Troll Queen why these were the requirements,

but she refused to answer him. If he'd known more than that, he might have been able to spare the poor girl living with him.

Still, he didn't want to end up as a bear forever. He wanted to return home to his people where they could feast like Scáthach and the warrior women were doing today.

More than anything else, Donnacha wanted to hug his brother again. He wanted to clap his hands on the shoulders of his cousins and family, to smell the salty earth of the mines, to dig with the rest of them and discover the most beautiful hidden treasures of the earth.

He missed being a dwarf. He missed his beard most of all, even though he had forgotten what his eyes looked like and the sound of his human voice. Not to mention his hands—

It wasn't worth entertaining the thought.

Scáthach was staring at him in complete shock. He hadn't thought he would startle her quite so much with the request.

Then she began to laugh. A roaring sound that shook through the rafters and sent a few pigeons fluttering into the air. "One of *my* warriors?"

"Yes."

"What has gotten into you?" She slapped a hand down on the table, laughing until tears streamed down her cheeks. "Do you really think I'm going to send one of my women with you? Away to Fuar Bheinn? Alone?"

He waited until she stopped laughing. It took a long time since Scáthach would pause laughing for a few moments, but then begin again when she looked at him. And so he waited. If nothing else, Donnacha was a patient man.

Finally, she wiped the tears from her face. "You're serious, aren't you?"

"Gravely."

"Why do you need one of my warrior women? You seem to be in fighting shape yourself."

"I don't need them to fight for me." He tried to convey his

reasoning with his gaze, but also knew very little emotion could be seen on his bear face. He couldn't imagine what this woman would think of his expression. Likely that he was snarling at her as a beast would.

"Then why do you need one?"

"I can't answer that."

She furrowed her brows. "You want me to send one of my women to your home, for reasons unknown, so you can do whatever you want with her?"

"They will be treated well. Given whatever they want in my castle."

"Castle now?" Scáthach tilted her head to the side and leveled him with a disbelieving look. "Since when do the dwarves have castles above ground?"

Since they were cursed by a Troll Queen who wanted him to marry her daughter. Since he hadn't been given a choice where he lived because the blasted woman wanted to keep track of him. These were all things he couldn't tell Scáthach, even though the truth burned in his chest.

Gruffly, he responded, "I can't tell you anything, Scáthach. You know the reason why."

He hoped at least. Most people knew that a curse could warp the tongue. She was a smart enough woman to be able to put the pieces together. He couldn't tell her, no matter how hard he tried.

Scáthach licked her lips. "What do we get in return?"

"Nothing."

"You want this for free then? Not even a favor to be called in at a later date?"

He shook his head. "I can't offer you anything in return."

"You want this out of the goodness of our hearts then?" She chuckled, leaning back in her chair and shaking her head. "This is a grave request for someone who has never done anything for my people."

"The legends of you have spread throughout the land,

Scáthach. You are a woman who enjoys helping others, someone who has created a legend of kindness and justice." He slowly stood from his place at her table. "It's my hope that you will continue that legend and assist someone who has begged for your help."

She watched him with a narrowed gaze. He didn't think she was questioning the truthfulness of his words. Instead, it seemed as though she were trying to weigh his soul.

"I will consider it," Scáthach replied. "Now leave my keep before I make you."

Nodding, he ambled out of the keep and back down into the training grounds. Would she keep her word? He had no way of knowing. Scáthach was an honorable woman, however, and he assumed she would at least consider it.

As he left the keep, his gaze shifted toward a particular headless strawman. The woman who had been standing there was gone, but the ghost of her remained. He still remembered the way the sunlight had bounced off the golden strands of her hair.

Would it be her? He highly doubted it. No one would spare such a capable woman when there were plenty of others who could be sacrificed to the beast of cold mountain.

Donnacha sighed and left Scáthach's renowned home. His feet found the path that would take him back to the castle. His long journey would start again.

He'd done what he could. He hoped someone would arrive in Fuar Bheinn someday soon, and his suffering could finally end.

3

"You want me to what?" Elva asked, forcing her body to remain still when she wanted to rush at the woman before her.

Scáthach had been the woman to teach her independence. She'd done more for Elva than her own mother, but somehow, this was still the woman who wanted to take away her independence again. And after all they'd done to coax Elva's mind to change. To tear her away from one terrible relationship, only to throw her to the wolves again.

Scáthach sighed, then nodded to the seat next to her at the head table. "Sit down, Elva. Let me explain."

"I don't want to sit."

"And yet, you will."

She knew better than to argue with Scáthach, but she wanted to. Oh, how she wanted to fly at the woman and scream in her face for daring to take away what she'd fought so hard to get. Her freedom meant more than anything else in this world.

Elva had struggled to gain every inch of this mindset. She had been so wrapped around Fionn's finger that she hadn't known who she was. Nor how to be a person who cared for herself even when other people needed her to be something different.

Gritting her teeth, Elva rounded the table and sat down next to Scáthach. If she hit the seat a little too hard, then it was merely because she'd been training all day, not because she was sulking. And certainly not because she was angry at the woman who wanted her to give up her life.

To a bear, of all things!

She didn't want to know why the creature had been in their camp. It didn't matter if he was cursed and needed her help. And she was certain that was the reason. Cursed creatures were easy to spot. They were like their animal brethren but…not. The bear had clearly been larger than any other creature she'd ever seen in the wild. His eyes were far too intelligent.

Scáthach pointed with a knife at the plate in front of Elva. "Eat."

"I don't want to eat."

"How many times are you going to defy me when I order you to do something, Elva? I'm not asking you to eat. I'm telling you to do so. Now close your mouth for a few minutes and open it only to put something between your lips. Understood?"

Not really, but Elva did what Scáthach asked. She reached forward and filled the plate with enough food to kill a horse. The training *had* made her hungry. Turkey, pig, and roasted squash on the table filled the air with aromas that made her mouth water. She wanted to devour everything in front of her, and would have if there weren't more pressing matters at hand.

She attacked the food with knife and fork as she would have liked to have done with the issue presented. Go with the bear? Live in his castle for a year and do…what? Elva had already lived a life where she wallowed in a palace with a faerie prince.

It hadn't ended well for either her or the prince.

Scáthach ate her own food in silence while she watched all the women in the hall. Her gaze lingered on the new women who had arrived, particularly on one whom Elva remembered had shown up more black and blue than skin colored.

"Do you know why I started this camp?" she asked.

Elva nodded. "Because you wanted all women to feel safe."

"That's what I tell people, and it's as good a lie as any other." Scáthach shrugged. "But that wasn't the reason. I started it because someone told me I couldn't be a warrior. They said women were meant to heal and to take care of the home. I never wanted that. I'd seen female warriors on the battlefield before. So I dedicated my life to becoming the best warrior to ever live. And then to teaching other women they, too, could be the same."

Elva wasn't certain where the story was going. What did this have to do with the bear? What did that have to do with asking Elva to leave the only place that felt like home?

"Scáthach—"

"I'm not finished yet." She waited until Elva fell silent before continuing. "These women show up on my door, battered, bruised, wanting to learn how to take revenge. Such teachings are not in my way. I will teach them to defend themselves, but I'm not going to help them destroy the thing that had nearly destroyed them.

"You arrived here as one of my most difficult protégés. You had a chip on your shoulder that even I had a hard time knocking out of you. But I succeeded. I gave you your life back. The one you wanted more than anything else in this world. Now, I'm asking you for something in return."

Elva had known there had to be a catch to this place. The first time she'd walked in and Scáthach had offered to help, she was certain this had to be some kind of faerie trick. But Scáthach wasn't a faerie. She was human. And, therefore, Elva *had* been tricked.

Her hackles rose. This was something she knew how to deal with. She'd grown up with women like this taking advantage of her. It still stung that someone she'd trusted with her entire being would betray her like this.

Setting down her fork, she cleared her throat. "Understood. I'm very familiar with favors."

"Not like this one." Scáthach glanced her way finally, her hand curling around the knife she held. "This bear asked for almost an exact description of you. Care to tell me why?"

"I don't know anyone who's cursed like that."

"Your family?"

"Also doesn't know anyone cursed. If they did, then they wouldn't be using that curse to get to me." Elva reached with her free hand and grabbed the goblet. The other, she slipped underneath the table, still clutching the knife.

"Are you certain of that?"

"I haven't talked to them in years, Scáthach. If they wanted to speak with me, they would have reached out. They could have reached out to my sister, to Bran, to the Seelie King. There are far more people who know more about me than you do. They wouldn't use a cursed bear to get me to come home."

Scáthach grunted and lifted her own goblet to her lips. "Then perhaps this is merely fate."

Elva didn't believe in fate. She believed in cause and effect. The bear asking for her in particular was troubling. Not a single person in her past would have stooped so low to ask one of the cursed to drag her back to the Seelie Court.

Who else could it be?

"Why was he asking for me?" Elva questioned.

"I couldn't get that out of him. I was hoping *you* would know." Scáthach shrugged. "I don't think it really matters in the end. You're going, whether you want to or not."

"To save a cursed bear? I could think of a few other things I'd rather be doing with my time."

"Saving? Whoever said anything about saving?"

Elva turned slowly toward her mentor and tried to figure out what the woman was getting at. Why else would she send Elva? She was the only person here who had firsthand experience with faerie curses. And it had to be a faerie who had cursed the bear.

She drew down her brows. "Why else would you send me? That curse reeks of fae magic, of which you know I have much experience with. You, of all people, know that I'm not just fae."

"Yes, your gift for the magical arts will likely help you with this, but I don't want you to save him. That bear… Well, I won't tell you who he is because that will only make this more difficult for you. Let's just say that his existence is not good for the faerie courts. Wandering fae without allegiance are dangerous, especially in the human realms."

"Scáthach," Elva said, her tones mocking in their surprise. "I didn't know you were involved in faerie politics."

"We're all involved in faerie politics, whether we want to be or not. This is the first opportunity in years that I have someone at my disposal who can actually be around one of the cursed faeries. Someone who knows the limitations of such a curse." She lifted her goblet into the air between them. "I want you to survey him. To learn what he knows, who he is, and how he came to be cursed. If he's a threat, I want you to destroy him."

"Why?"

"He shares land with my people. I don't trust men. More than that, I don't trust people who waltz into my keep and demand that I assist them. Find out what you can and then return here to me. If he gives you any reason to think he's dangerous to us or to this land, destroy him."

"How do you want me to destroy a bear?" There were a few ways she could think of, and none of them that Scáthach would support. She hated magic and everything it promised.

"With whatever means necessary. I think you'll find I'm far more generous with those who play by my games, Elva, than those who don't. You've had a home here, and we welcomed you back even after you saved your sister. I don't like faeries. I don't like magic. And I really don't like liars. You have taken an oath to serve me. Now serve."

The order shouldn't have smarted as much as it did. Elva had been born into a high-ranking faerie family. They were the ones who gave orders, not some human who thought she was high and mighty.

But that was the old Elva, the one who valued people on the age of their blood and how much they could offer her. Now, she understood how much hard work went into the lives of the commoners. She valued them for what they could do, not for who they were.

Elva reminded herself she wasn't the same person she had been. She wasn't some spoiled princess who thought the world should bow at her feet.

She couldn't be. Not anymore.

Arguing at this point was ridiculous. Instead, she watched her fellow warriors feast at the table. Their lives were better because Scáthach existed. This woman had taken in so many people out of the goodness of her heart. She'd taught women how to take care of themselves, and how to fight if necessary.

In a way, Elva did owe her. The binds of that realization tightened around her chest. A faerie didn't like owing anyone anything. It was a physical restraint that made it nearly impossible for her to do anything or be anyone other than the little slave girl Scáthach wanted her to be. Whatever the human asked, Elva would do.

Her lip curled. "Fine, I'll do it. But once this is over, our bonds are severed for good."

"You want to go home?"

No, of course she didn't want to go home. Back at her parents' house, she would become some flowering, simpering thing who didn't have a real bone in her body. She had been a fluid creature who became whatever anyone else wanted her to be.

The idea of becoming that again made her sick to her stomach.

And Elva didn't question that she would turn right back down that same path.

She'd tried returning home, right after Fionn had been banished. It hadn't gone well. Her mother had brought out all her old dresses, the ones that made her feel like a doll. They'd thrown party after party, trying to get the old suitors to look her over again.

All they had managed to do was make her feel like a prized cow. When the newest suitor tried to kiss her without permission, Elva had headbutted him so hard she'd nearly knocked herself out.

The snapping of the man's nose, however, was an accomplishment she'd wear forever as a badge of pride. That had been the moment she realized she didn't want to be Elva, the pretty noble who needed a man to be her husband. She wanted to be feared. To be a woman who could take care of herself without someone standing between her and life.

So she'd come here, to Scáthach's island where they made women warriors. Where she could be someone else because no one knew she was faerie royalty.

Other than Scáthach. This woman knew she was a faerie, knew her entire story, and it seemed she might use that knowledge against her.

Elva blew out a breath. Did she want to leave this life behind? No. She didn't want to go home and she didn't want to return to the faerie courts where everyone knew her as a prideful woman who wanted a husband. She wanted to stay on this isle where everyone else understood the pain in her chest.

But she couldn't stay here and continue to owe this woman an arm and a leg. She had to make her own way in life. And that was that.

"I won't return home," she replied. "There are other places I can go."

"Like where?" Scáthach speared a radish with her knife and

popped it in her mouth. Talking over the food, she asked, "Your sister's kingdom?"

She didn't want to go to Underhill with all its monstrous creatures, although Bran was there and she considered him her oldest friend. Her sister had reasons to not want her in the kingdom, however. Bran and Elva had been engaged and…well, it was best to avoid that conflict.

Elva shrugged. "There are places in the faerie courts who would be interested in having me."

"Believe that if you want to. I think you'll find it's harder to get them to accept you once you leave this place." Scáthach toasted her and drank the ale down, then slammed the goblet onto the table. "To new adventures and a debt repaid."

Elva flinched. "To debts repaid."

4

The journey home was far shorter than he would have liked. Donnacha enjoyed his time away from the icy castle of his home. At least he wasn't within the clutches of the Troll Queen.

Shaking his great head, he stared up at the monolith she'd given him. Pillars of ice stretched up into the sky like giant swords. The entire castle glimmered in the sunlight, shining like diamonds. Even the windows were made of stained glass, a testament to the wealth of whomever built it.

She'd created it thinking he would thank her for such a ridiculous home. Dwarves liked wealth, she had told him. He should appreciate the gift she'd given him.

But he didn't. All Donnacha wanted was a normal life. One where he could be mining away with the rest of his family. Instead of kidnapped and cursed by a Troll Queen.

The memory of his curse burned in the back of his mind, always trying to draw his attention away from anything else. He'd been wandering in the forest, a place he shouldn't have been, when the Troll Queen and her entourage first saw him.

The dwarves had known the trolls were coming. All others had hidden themselves away, but Donnacha liked to think himself brave. The troll princess had set her eyes on him and decided he was all she wanted. She would have him and no one else. And so, the Troll Queen had offered him a choice.

Marry her daughter that instant, or be cursed as a bear until he gave in.

He didn't want to marry her daughter. He didn't want to be cursed in this form because of some game she thought was entertaining. Most of all, he wanted to go home. Back under the ground where the dwarves didn't care about shiny things. They cared only for each other and the families they had built.

Shaking his great head, he started up the icy stairs. Human feet would have had a hard time with the trek. Though beautiful, the stairs weren't created with ease in mind. They were far too slippery for booted feet. Even Donnacha, with his claws that dug into the ice, had a difficult time getting up to the castle doors.

Or maybe that was his gut telling him to slow down just a little bit. He wasn't in any rush to return to the cold castle with its empty halls. The wind whistled through the castle at night, whipping through the nooks and crannies until it sounded like the building itself was screaming.

The double doors, carved with hunters and the beasts they killed, opened at his approach. The Troll Queen had been thorough in her curse and his new home. Everything in it was spelled to have a mind of its own. The castle frequently did what he wanted without being asked.

If only it could break the curse as well.

He snarled at the doors as he went through. The first few times they'd opened on their own, he had broken them in a fit of rage. The next day, they were exactly the same way as they had been before. Not a crack or a change in the carvings at all. As if his anger hadn't happened.

Donnacha desperately wanted something in this place to change. But it never did. No matter how many times his claws dug into the ice floors, the marks were gone the next day. It was as if he didn't exist at all.

Perhaps he didn't anymore. No one else could hear the ghosts whispering in his lungs, the old voices and songs of his people that he couldn't sing while his body was trapped as a beast.

His memories were his only solace. The old times when he had gathered with his dwarven brothers and sisters, singing the old songs, in caverns where their voices had lifted to the ceiling and bounced from stone to stone.

He could still hear them if he listened closely enough. He could hear their voices that sounded like angels, the cascade of emotion that would rain down upon them as they sang of ancestors who had dug deep into the earth and found treasures of legend.

"You've returned." The voice fluttered through the blue halls and sent a shiver down his spine. "You're late."

He didn't want to respond. Gods, what he would give if he could just go back to his room with its comfortable pile of furs and hide from what he had to do.

But he couldn't. The curse made certain of that.

Donnacha padded through the halls, avoiding snow drifts as he made his way toward the one room that he hated more than anything else. At the farthest western point of the castle, a door opened for him.

This was the only door not made of glimmering ice. All the others revealed the insides of the rooms, wavering lines of what was beyond, not quite enough to make out who or what was hiding within the castle, but enough to see something moving when he passed. There was never anything moving.

Instead, this door was made of black stone. The obsidian reflected his own image as he approached the smooth surface. It swung open silently.

He knew what this meant, why that gravel-toned voice was calling for him. The queen wanted to know whether or not he was successful. Lip curling in anger and defeat, he stepped into the shadowy room beyond.

There was nothing but a single mirror in the room. Tall as three men, it was an impressive sight to most. The ornate frame was made of more black stone. The carved swirls had been made by the most talented of dwarven hands.

She thought it entertaining to visit him in something his own ancestors had created.

The smooth mirror surface swirled with magic, sickly green light pouring out until it stilled into something that looked more like a window. He didn't want to look. He didn't want to see the creature who awaited him.

Donnacha remembered her appearance as though he had seen her just yesterday. He didn't need to gaze upon her monstrous form again. The curse tightened around his throat, making him stare up at the mirror.

The Troll Queen stood before him. Her skin was a disgusting blueish gray, the same as the slate he'd mined when he was just a child learning how to use a pickaxe. Her eyes were too large for her face and entirely black. Her flattened nose made her look more animal-like than the others. Her overly large mouth curved into a smile, revealing sharpened teeth he knew she had filed long ago. Her ears were pressed flat against her skull, set too high for a human face, and twig-like hair was severely pulled back from her face.

He wished he could say her body was at least mildly attractive, but it wasn't. She looked like a skeletal mix between a wraith and a banshee. Too thin for health, but somehow still clinging to life.

She wore nothing more than a white gown. It hung from her frame like someone had forgotten a coat on a hanger, and it had aged beyond recognition. Although, she didn't care what she looked like. The Troll Queen cared for nothing other than her own daughter, a creature even more monstrous than she was.

Her smile split wider as she watched his disgusted reaction. "You aren't happy to see me, dwarven noble? I'm insulted."

"Good. I wouldn't want you to believe for even a moment I was pleased to see you."

"Oh, little dwarf. Are you angry at me?"

"Of course, I'm angry at you. It's a permanent state of being," Donnacha growled in response.

She knew this already, but liked to poke at him. Quite literally poking the bear. She wanted to see him angry, and she wanted to know he was suffering in this life she'd created for him. This prison made of glorious ice and stone.

If Donnacha could have killed her, he would have. But the Troll Queen was smarter than to let that happen, something he couldn't say for her daughter. While the offspring was dumb and slow, the mother knew how to work a curse. She'd never let either of them get close enough for him to touch. Always a barrier of glass stood between them.

He lifted a lip in anger. "What do you want?"

"You met with the warrior women?"

"I did. You already know this, Queen."

She lifted a hand and touched her hair. The straw strands shifted under her touch as she moved a single one back into place. It was so brittle it rattled when she touched it. "Were they angry at you? Did they threaten to kill you like I thought they would?"

"If I die, the curse is broken."

"I wouldn't let you die. I have bigger plans for you, Donnacha. You know that. So? Did they threaten you?"

He dug his claws into the ice. "Is that what your plan was? Do you desire some reason to end them? To attack them?"

"I have no interest in mortal women."

"Then why ask me to bring one here?"

She looked down at her nails, holding them in front of her as if admiring the ragged ends. "I didn't ask you to bring a mortal woman here. I asked you bring one with hair like sunlight, whose anger rivals the sun itself. A warrior woman better than all the mortal women in that camp."

"They're all mortal women."

"Except one." The Troll Queen laughed. "You already saw her, didn't you? I doubt you could miss the pretty thing."

Was she talking about the woman who had cleaved the head from the strawman? He couldn't imagine what she'd want with a woman like that. The warrior was nothing more than mortal. He would have known if she was a dwarf, and she was too tall besides.

His mind stalled out when he realized what she was hinting at. "Did you have me bargain for a Seelie Fae to come here?"

The laughter bubbling out of the Troll Queen's mouth was almost pretty if he didn't know what it meant. "Of course, I did! Isn't that entertaining?"

Oh, gods. He couldn't breathe. His lungs seized up in horror at what she'd had him do, and his heart started beating so quickly he thought it might rattle out of his chest. A Seelie Fae? She'd had him make a bargain for a Seelie Fae?

He knew what that meant. Faeries weren't kind, especially those of the royal line. They wouldn't let something like that go unnoticed. They would hunt him down. Destroy everything he was, his family, his lineage. Donnacha would be wiped from this realm so thoroughly no one would even remember his name.

He looked at the mirror in horror and croaked, "What have you done?"

"I made certain you will never be able to renounce my daughter. The trolls are the only ones who can save you now, dwarf. You might as well accept defeat and come live with us. Otherwise, the faeries will hunt you down."

"You've signed my life away to the courts," he growled.

"All you have to do is marry my daughter, and you'll be safe."

No! He didn't want to marry her daughter. He wanted nothing to do with the beastly creature who would make his life hell. But the choice had been stripped from his hands now that his family was involved.

The faerie courts didn't care about him. They didn't care about his family. They only cared about a deal gone bad, and that meant he was going to need to do something about this.

He had to beg the faerie woman not to seek retribution. He would have to return to the camp on his hands and knees, praying she would see reason when he explained what had happened—the Troll Queen was the one who had made him ask for her. He didn't care if she came to this ice castle and changed her life to help him.

Donnacha opened his mouth to say this to the Queen, only to be interrupted.

"Dwarf, do you really think I don't know where you mind will travel? Do you think for even a second I don't know how that brain of yours works? You aren't allowed to leave the castle grounds for the next year. That is the deal. You wanted to go and seek something that would help break the curse, didn't you?"

She'd completely ruined any chance of fixing this. He slumped, sitting on the cold ice his head hanging. "She can't come here. They will follow her."

"I doubt a little Seelie Fae will come all the way to Fuar Bheinn just for you. And if she does, then she'll run very quickly." The Troll Queen clapped her hands gleefully. "Oh, Donnacha! This was so much fun! You actually thought you could break the curse, didn't you?"

Her laughter rang in his ears. He stared at the floor, horrified that he'd fallen under her spell yet again.

He had thought the curse could be broken. Hope had bloomed in his chest, and that emotion was more dangerous than rage or wrath could ever be. He'd thought… Gods, he'd thought he could do something more than just be stuck in this body as a bear with a Troll Princess as his intended bride.

His life wasn't anything like he'd imagined. As a boy, he'd thought mining was his future. That someday he would take his father's place and create beautiful instruments made of gold and silver ore. He'd thought life would be more than just disgust at himself, at the creatures who had cursed him, at the future barreling toward him with nothing to stop it.

"Come now, Donnacha, you'll insult me. My daughter is the greatest creature to ever live, and you are the one who is going to marry her. Be a little happier, or I'll find it an insult."

He couldn't be happy. How could he be happy when he knew a troll would await him in the marriage bed? That he'd have to…

Donnacha gagged.

The Troll Queen snapped at him, her mouth opening wider than should be possible and sharpened teeth flashing. "Careful, dwarf. You might anger me."

A flash of magic filled the room, and then the Troll Queen was gone. The mirror reflected only his own dejected stance.

What was he going to do? The faerie woman wasn't going to come here, of all places. She didn't even know *why* he had summoned her here. And she never would because he couldn't say a single word about how he'd turned into a bear or why this castle had appeared out of thin air.

He should give up now and go with the trolls. Yet something in him refused to relent so easily. He couldn't, not yet.

Donnacha had to put his faith in a faerie noble. He huffed out a breath, stood, and made his way to his own room. There wasn't a single fiber in him that believed she'd come here. Why would she?

Faeries didn't care about anyone other than themselves.

5

Elva brushed a branch away from her face, snarling as it tangled in her hair. *Go to the bear's home,* Scáthach had ordered. *Find him, watch him, learn if he's the dangerous creature they all seem to think he is*. And if he was? *Kill him.*

Right. Just kill the bear.

That was supposed to be the hardest part of this mission. Not journeying through the forest with all the faerie creatures trying to distract her. Not the trees that snarled in her hair and clothes, nor the branches that tried to rip her hair from the root. And it certainly wasn't supposed to be her own frustration, telling her to get out of the forest now and let the humans deal with their own messes.

She grunted as another branch smacked her in the face. "Fine, that's it."

Elva drew her blade and started hacking at everything that stood in her way. The trees were supposed to be honored, sure. Their roots were deep in the ground, and they'd struggled to survive for years. If they wanted to stand on their own, then they shouldn't have been hitting her. Every strike made her feel better, anyways. The chip on her shoulder had only grown.

She was a damned faerie princess, or had been. Why had she been the one forced to go? There were plenty of other warrior women who could have done this. They were human, besides. They would have been a better choice to save one of their own. Not the faerie woman who didn't like humans that much.

Elva tolerated them. Humans were foolish creatures through and through, and she thought them rather pitiful. They needed guidance more than they needed help, but that didn't mean she wanted to save the lot of them. And the bear had to be human. No faerie would have let himself get so foolishly cursed. Faerie royals were cursed by politicians who moved to take thrones with complex rules and years of study required. Shapeshifting curses were far too easy.

Tree limbs snapped in front of her, nearly hiding the sound of laughter on the wind. The last thing she needed was another faerie seeing her struggle. They'd likely run back to the courts to tell them Elva was on the loose again.

Not that anyone would come for her. She'd made it very clear that no one was to disturb her on this journey in finding herself. Even her mother had been afraid the last time they'd gotten into a screaming match. With all the changes that had happened, killing her own mother didn't seem like such a stretch. She'd told the woman that to her face.

Elva still savored the memory of her mother's face whitening in fear. After all that had happened, she wasn't surprised her mother believed her. This was the same woman who had pushed her into perfection. The same woman who had sent her sister away to the human realm to be a changeling because she was a little different. Because the Raven King wanted Aisling for his own. Instead of protecting her own child, their parents had discarded her like dirty laundry.

Enough was enough. She wanted nothing to do with the faerie courts or their back-stabbing ways. Elva was a new person. She would live with the humans if that was what it took, but she was done making deals with other faeries.

The giggles started up again, and another branch whacked her in the face.

"Let me warn you," she said, letting the wind carry her words, "I have no interest in speaking with others of our kind. If you try to tempt me off the path, I will not follow. If you try to sway me, I will not listen."

The giggles continued, almost as if the faerie didn't believe her.

She twisted her hand on the grip of her blade. Fighting something else would let off a little steam, although she had a feeling it wasn't something strong out in the forest. If it were a powerful fae, then it would have attacked her already. Instead, it hid.

Elva slanted her eyes to the side when a twig snapped. A dark piece of fabric shifted in the shadows and then seemed to disappear.

"Come out," she called, "and I'll let you live."

Another giggle from her left. "That's not for you to say, faerie. That's for the master of the mountain to decide."

"Where do you think I'm heading?" she asked.

"Not to Fuar Bheinn. No one wants to go there."

"Maybe I do." She turned in a slow circle, watching the shadows for anything that looked remotely like a faerie. Hunting in forests was always difficult. Everything looked like a faerie in the right light.

"Why would you want to go there? There's nothing but ice and snow."

"Yes, I've heard it's cold."

"It's more than cold. It's a veritable freezing fortress, and no one who goes there comes out quite the same."

"Is that so?" Elva asked, watching a particular place in the shadows where she was certain the creature was hiding. "Why do you think that? Have you been there before?"

"You're really set on going there?" Another giggle drifted on the wind. "That's a shame. You're very beautiful."

She hated those words more than anything else. Call her intimidating. Call her something more than just beautiful, more than just something that was pretty to put on a shelf as she'd been so many times in her life. "If you know where it is, then perhaps you'll show me how to get there."

"Why would we do that?"

"We?" Elva flashed a grin. "Good to know there's more than one of you."

The swift sound of a slap followed her declaration. She heard them whispering together, pinpointing that there had to only be two of them. Small blessing. Dealing with more than one wandering faerie was already going to be a pain in her royal rump, let alone a handful of them.

Finally, one of the faeries spoke up again. "If we show you where to go, what will you give us in return?"

Elva chuckled. "I'm not dealing with you, fae. If you want to help me, then help. I offer nothing in return."

"Then why would we help?"

They had a point. Faeries weren't likely to help her at all if she didn't give them something in return. They were notoriously unhelpful creatures. And wasn't she just following in their footsteps if she didn't offer something up?

She was dealing with faeries already, even when she said she would never do that again.

Elva snarled. "Fine, what do you want?"

An ugly face poked out of the brush. Lined with age and so furrowed, it looked like a dog she'd seen once in a human home. The wrinkles sagged down over eyes that were barely visible and a mouth that was puckered. "A kiss perhaps?"

Before she had time to even respond to that ridiculous request, a gnarled hand reached out above its head and smacked it on the crown. "How dare you!"

The head retracted back into the thorns, and it appeared the two creatures began to fight. She could hear them rustling and swearing in the distance.

This wasn't getting her anywhere. A bodach and cailleach bride? The faeries were hardly more than fools, ancient things who had grown so old and decrepit they didn't know which way was up and which way was down. She'd heard of them before, but never had the misfortune of meeting one in person. They were notorious for throwing travelers off their path so they wandered.

Elva stooped down and pulled the brush aside. The two faeries were tangled around each other, both the size of a small dog. Moldy fabric covered their bodies, ugly green and black mold puffed into the air as they tore at each other.

"You said you loved me!"

"I do!"

"But you wanted her to kiss you? I ought to take off your eyebrows!"

"Not my eyebrows!" the one who had to be male said. "I just got 'em to stick on!"

They rolled close enough to Elva for her to snatch the back of their jackets and pull them apart. Holding each at arm's length, she waited until they stopped twisting in her arms.

The female kicked her feet. "Let me down!" she shrieked.

Elva sighed heavily and told herself to remain calm. If she had believed the gods were anything more than grandparents, she would have prayed to them for some kind of patience. As it was, it took her to a count of ten before her temper calmed down.

The bodach was still trying to reach her hand where she held him. "Faerie woman, put me down," he shouted.

"Not a chance."

"We had a deal!"

Elva leaned closer to him, eyes narrowed and jaw tight. "We didn't make any kind of deal. Let's make that very clear. Now, it seems like I have a deal to make with you. I'll put you down, unharmed, if you tell me which way the castle is."

He pointed behind them. "That way."

She was seventy percent sure he was lying to her. Or perhaps not lying, but that path would take her months to reach the castle. Technically, any way he pointed was the right way. If she had to walk around the entire Earth to get to the castle, which could take a lifetime, it was still a path that would take her there.

Elva looked to the cailleach in her other hand. "And you? Which way is the castle?"

The female faerie pointed in the opposite direction.

Oh, she was going to destroy them. Elva took a deep breath and looked up at the heavens as if they might help. She didn't want to hurt another faerie. It felt wrong. But she also didn't know how to make them talk.

Without looking at either faerie—if she looked then she was going to really hurt them—she said, "I'm going to give you one more chance. Both of you tell me where the castle is, where it *really* is, and I won't throw you so far you learn what bird's feel like before you hit the ground."

"I don't think you'd do that," the bodach replied.

Elva let all her rage seep into her eyes. She squared her jaw and squeezed the fabric in both hands, twisting until the faeries grasped at their throats. She waited until their faces turned red before she snarled, "Please, try me."

Releasing her hold enough so they could breathe, she watched as they tried to get their bearings. They had no idea who they were dealing with.

And that wasn't kind of her, now was it? She tilted her head to the side when they didn't speak immediately. "Do you know who I am?"

"A faerie witch," the cailleach grunted. "Put us down, now!"

"Oh no no. I'm not a faerie witch. I'm the wife of the first Seelie King. Fionn the Magnificent, I believe he made everyone call him. I was there when he was dethroned. I was there when he was banished. And yes, I did help the King of Underhill take back his throne, find his wife, and kill Carmen, the mother of all witches." She brought them both closer to her face. "Do you really want to see what I can do with two little faeries in a forest so far away from anyone? No one will hear you scream."

The bodach swallowed audibly. "The castle is that way." He pointed the way his wife had originally pointed. "Follow the path."

"I don't think I trust either of you."

"I wouldn't lead you wrong, mistress."

Elva arched a brow.

He swallowed again. "Highness."

"I want to clarify, bodach"— she nodded at the woman in her other hand—"cailleach. If you have pointed me in the wrong direction, I will come back here. Don't think you can run from me. I've hunted things larger than you and far smarter than you. I will come back. I will find you. And when I do, I am going to rip every single hair from your body, pull out all your fingernails, and feed you to my wolves. Understood?"

The bodach nodded. "Yes, highness."

She looked at the cailleach. "And you?"

The woman eyed her and frowned. "We're here to watch the forest. We make sure no one gets to the castle, even the ones who want to get there. That's our job, miss."

"Is it? And who employs you?"

Shaking her head, the cailleach replied, "Can't tell you, miss."

"Can't or won't?"

"Can't."

Which meant it was a particularly powerful faerie who had employed them. This place had just gotten significantly more interesting. Elva shook the cailleach a little. "Why don't you make my journey a little faster then?"

The sullen look on the cailleach's face made it clear she wanted to deny Elva's request. The faerie didn't want to help Elva at all. Although, she really couldn't blame the tiny faerie. Elva was holding her by the shirt collar.

Raising a hand, the cailleach snapped her fingers. A great swirl of movement made the entire forest shift under Elva's feet. It appeared as though she was moving at a great speed, or perhaps the forest was moving on its own, but she was standing still.

Senses whirling, she held onto the faeries for dear life until the movement stopped. Her breath came in ragged gasps as she looked at her new surroundings.

A castle towered above her. Ice pillars gleamed in the sunlight. Stained glass windows cast rainbows across at least ten towers that were both beautiful and wickedly dangerous.

She swallowed. "So this is Fuar Bheinn then?"

The bodach snorted. "You've been walking in Fuar Bheinn for hours. *That* is the ice palace."

"Ah. Home to the cursed bear, I assume?"

The cailleach shivered in her grasp, then nodded. "The beast of Fuar Bheinn."

Interesting that the faeries were afraid of him. She hadn't seen any reason for such a visceral reaction to the creature. The bear was certainly a problem. He was powerful and capable of doing much harm, considering there was a human mind inside such a beast. But that didn't make him frightening. Only the soul inside the creature could be that terrifying.

She stared at the ice stairs and sighed. That was going to take her a while to maneuver, and she hadn't really expected to deal with climbing this early in the trek.

Deirdre had been right. Fuar Bheinn created its own kind of cold that frosted the air and made her breath puff in front of her face.

"Thanks for the help," she muttered, then tossed the faeries onto the ground. "Now, off with you."

The bodach helped the cailleach up, dusting off her backside and making snide comments about faeries with fat heads. "We won't help you again, you know," he muttered.

"I think you won't have a choice if I need help again."

"Try us."

Elva turned around and placed a hand on her sword. "Try *me*, faerie."

He snarled. The little thing could probably bite, but he was so old, chances were he'd end up only gumming her. Elva didn't have time to deal with ridiculous faeries who didn't know a Tuatha de Danann when they saw one. They wouldn't even be allowed into the courts if they tried to enter.

When they were far enough away that she knew they couldn't bother her anymore, Elva set her pack onto the ground. She flexed her shoulders to try to rid herself of the discomfort. It had been a long time since she'd traveled like this. Perhaps too long considering the stiffness in her back and neck.

Rubbing the muscles, she reached into her pack and pulled out the straps for her boots. Small nails had been hammered through the leather. It wasn't much, but it would help her grip onto the ice.

A few moments later, she was ready to try this next piece of the journey. The castle looked faerie made, she mused as she picked up her pack again.

The nails in her boots sank into the ice like claws. It was slow going; she had to make sure every step counted. But she wasn't in any rush to get to the castle. Elva wasn't particularly proud of her reluctance. This was going to get rid of her last debt, the last lingering thing that weighed heavy on her soul. She should be a lot happier to be doing this.

Instead, dread made her stomach churn. She wasn't going to like any part of this journey. Every step felt like she was going toward something that would change her life forever.

And that was a foolish thought. It was just a man cursed as a bear, but that didn't mean he was going to hurt her. He couldn't. She was a faerie, and he was just a human man. If she wanted to tear his head from his body, she could.

Step by step, she made her way toward the castle. It was a rather beautiful structure. The stained-glass windows looked like something out of a fairytale, the human kind of course, not the faerie ones.

Elva looked up every now and then, pausing to adjust the straps on her shoulders and wondering why she wasn't getting up the stairs faster. She started counting each step. Sometimes she stopped to count the steps ahead as well.

It seemed as though for every ten steps up, she only traveled one.

Gods, she hated cursed places like this. The bear wasn't the only one under a spell then; it was the entire kingdom. She should have guessed that from the cold air. Something didn't want her to make it to the castle.

The bonds she'd promised to Scáthach tightened around her throat. She had to make it to the castle. She'd said that she would, which meant she had to.

So she continued up and up. Her thighs started to burn. She grit her teeth against the discomfort and decided it was good to work the muscles of her body. Elva had trained an entire lifetime, it seemed, in that camp with Scáthach and the other warrior women. Now, she got to use that to her benefit.

Finally, there was only one step left. She took it two at a time, counting until ten was over. When her foot reached the top of the stairwell leading into the castle, she let out a breath of relief. One more step down. Now, all she had to do was find the bear.

A deep, rumbling voice interrupted her. Inhuman in its quality, it was equal part voice and growl as it burst through her thoughts. "So, you made it. Impressive."

She looked up, hands squeezing the straps at her shoulders so she didn't draw her blade. The bear stood in front of her. His head was tilted to the side as he watched her, and his shoulders were hunched as though he was trying to make himself smaller.

He needn't try. No matter how curled into his body he drew himself, he'd always be something monstrous and terrifying in size.

The brown hair covering his body appeared much less coarse this close up. It almost appeared soft, although she didn't want the thought to linger too long. He wasn't a creature she could find fascinating. He was an animal she needed to watch and make certain he wasn't evil.

Her grip made the leather at her shoulders creak. "Wasn't that much of a struggle."

"Most find it to be."

He was watching her, as if he expected her to react somehow. What did he want? Her to run screaming from his visage? She wasn't that kind of woman.

Elva waited for him to say something more. Or stand aside so she could enter the castle. Instead, he stood in the doorway, staring at her.

Say something, she wanted to shout at him. He couldn't remain quiet the entire time, staring at her like some kind of fool. He had thoughts in his head. She could see them dancing behind those dark eyes. He had words since she'd already heard him. So why was he just… staring?

Elva cleared her throat. "My name is Elva. Scáthach sent me—"

"I know."

She started. Had he just interrupted her? "She sent me to—"

"Yes, I'm aware."

An angry breath escaped her before she could suck it back into her lungs. "Then perhaps you can tell me why you sent for me?"

"I didn't send for you." He shuffled his feet, the long claws scraping the ice.

"You asked for someone who looks remarkably like me then."

"Perhaps." The bear finally tore his gaze away from her. He looked down at her feet, then at his own before a ragged chuff escaped him. "Remarkable, indeed."

Was he looking at her boots? Surely he wasn't one of those men who had a ridiculous fetish, and all of a sudden he'd be asking to smell her shoes. She'd already dealt with one of those at the palace, not the king of course, but a lesser known fae who had been known to sneak her slippers out of the room for "private time."

Disgusted at the thought, Elva looked down at her boots and blurted out, "My shoes?"

"Well, yes. They are rather remarkable, don't you think?"

"Not at all."

He blinked a few times at the ground then looked up at her. "I know very few women who would have the wherewithal to affix nails to their shoes."

Heat rushed to her face. He was talking about the *nails?* She'd never been more embarrassed in her life and more thoroughly pleased she'd learned how to keep her mouth shut. "Ah." Elva cleared her throat. "Right. The straps."

The bear's eyes glittered with mirth. "The straps," he agreed.

Oh, god, she was going to melt the ice if her temperature went up any higher. She hadn't been embarrassed around a man in... She couldn't remember. Elva made it a point to always put her best foot forward with them. To be an intimidating woman who let no one through her barriers. Not even those who were closest to her. And here this man had already made her think about foot fetishes.

"You asked me to come here," she started again, hoping he'd let her get away with it this time. "Don't try to distract me. You clearly asked specifically, and I would like to know why."

If a bear could grin, he did. Then, he turned away from her and started walking down a hall made entirely of blue ice. "Come along, faerie. I'll show you where you'll be staying. I'm sure you're tired after such a long journey."

She wasn't, but he didn't need to know that. Let him think she was a weak woman. It would make everything she might have to do that much easier. Elva followed him silently down the hall and marveled at the magical place he lived.

She looked around at the beauty and tried not to be too

impressed. It was difficult when magic had clearly carved the entire building with a hand that knew true beauty. The floor, walls, and ceiling were glass-like in their pristine smoothness. There was something effortless in the glamour.

She suddenly was sad her feet had nails on them. Wherever she walked, this place would be marked. And it wasn't a place meant to be marked by the likes of her.

Maybe it wasn't really ice. Elva reached out and trailed her fingers along the wall. They were slick with water when she pulled them away, just as suddenly freezing as the cold air frosted them.

"I wouldn't touch it too much," the bear grumbled ahead of her.

How had he seen her touch it? Raising a brow, she pulled her dignity around her as she tucked her hand back into its sleeve. "Why not?"

"The castle has a way of healing itself. I wouldn't want your finger getting stuck as it rebuilt the ice." Was it humor she heard in his voice? Or was he simply being gruff?

Elva didn't know what to think of this creature as she padded behind him. Scáthach made it seem as though he were some cursed man, the kind who deserved what he got. Yet he didn't seem like the kind of man who would provoke the direst of magics. He seemed…kind.

The bear stopped in front of a door and held his paw out toward the carved ice. "This is yours."

She peered through the ice, seeing only colored shadows beyond. "You can see right through the walls."

"You needn't worry. This isn't a part of the castle I frequent often."

Why wouldn't he want to be around her? He'd asked for her to be here, hadn't he? She blew out a breath and turned full toward him. "You want to hide me away?"

"If possible."

"Why ask me to come here then?" Not to mention it would force her to go against what she'd promised Scáthach. She had to be around him to figure out whether or not he was a good person or a threat to the warrior women.

The bear shrugged. "I hope you enjoy your time here. I regret that it is as long as it must be. However, this place will provide for you."

"This place?" she repeated as he turned around. "Does anyone else live here?"

The bear didn't stop. Instead, he tossed words over his shoulder as he retreated. "No. It's just me."

He rounded a corner and was then gone from her sight. She couldn't even hear his nails clicking on the ice floors.

What in the world had she gotten herself into? Elva hefted her pack over her shoulder more firmly and pushed the door open with her back. She was going to have to make more straps like this. The boots she wore now were good for travel, but they'd quickly blister her feet. Anything else, and she'd slip on the floors and likely not be able to get up again.

She turned into the room and stopped. Shock nearly made her jaw drop open.

Ice pillars created a masterpiece of a bed. Four posters anchored into the floor and ceiling. The frame of the bed was made of white ice, swirled with bubbles like a raging waterfall had frozen in place. Furs were piled high in the center and what looked like a mattress was beneath them.

No fireplace. No candles. Nothing to heat up the room as the sun dipped below the horizon.

In fact, there was nothing else in the room at all. Just the bed and ice walls.

Perhaps that was the bear's motive. He was going to freeze her to death. She'd wake up in the morning with her eyelashes frozen shut and the great beast gnawing on her leg.

The mere idea made shivers dance down her spine. Or

perhaps that was simply the cold finally getting to her. She hadn't brought nearly enough warm clothes for this. But then again, Elva didn't *have* that many warm clothes. She was from the warmest part of the faerie realm. Her own belongings were made for sun-drenched revelries.

Sighing, she tossed her pack onto the ground beside the bed. The furs called out to her, but she wanted to explore a little more before she was tempted to let the warmth sink into her bones. There was something going on in this castle, and she needed to find out.

Elva watched the ice walls for movement. Seeing nothing beyond, she tiptoed to the door and opened it slightly.

"Wouldn't do that if I were you." The voice came from the other side of the ice. Even though she hadn't seen anyone just a second ago, now, there was a smudge of darkness directly in front of her door.

This wasn't the bear, yet he'd said no one else inhabited the castle.

Elva furrowed her brows. "And you are?"

"Clurichaun."

The creature needed to say no more to make sure she stayed in her room. A clurichaun? Really? The bear kept poor company. First the bodach and cailleach, ancient buffoons who were simply a waste of time, and now this? She thought leprechauns were bad.

Clurichaun were nothing more than the drunkard cousins of the gold-obsessed faeries. Instead of spending their time creating pots of gold, hunting down the shiniest objects they could find, the clurichaun spent every hour of the day drinking their lives away.

Elva's shoulders curved forward in defeat. "Why shouldn't I leave the room?"

"Nighttime is dangerous in the castle."

"The sun isn't setting." A sudden waft of cold air pushed through the door, and she realized the light *had* gone down. All of a sudden. But she'd most certainly seen the sun when she walked up the stairs, and it had still been high in the sky when she entered the castle. It wasn't possible for it to be setting so soon.

The clurichaun poked his head in the gap between the door. He was a short, squat fellow. A shock of red hair tufted into a mohawk at his crown, and his cheeks were ruddy with drink. He came up to about her waist, what she expected was rather tall for one of his species, and his legs were far shorter than his torso.

"Sure, it isn't," he grumbled, squinting up at her. "This castle has a way of making its own weather, you see. I'd suggest you get under the covers."

"And if I don't?"

"I'm just telling you what's safest, miss."

She frowned at the small creature as he started away from her. Elva called out, "The master of this castle said no one else lived here."

The clurichaun froze. "What he doesn't know won't hurt him."

"I think he'd have a different opinion."

When the faerie turned around, she realized he was clutching three bottles of liquid in his arms. Wine? She hadn't imbibed in any since her time in the faerie courts. Humans didn't have an abundance of the rare stuff. Not these days.

He watched her with narrowed eyes before he finally harrumphed. "What do you want?"

She held out her hand.

"No."

Elva wriggled her fingers.

"Absolutely not."

"Then I'll just let the master know you've been raiding his storehouses. I'm sure the bear won't mind at all that a strange faerie has been living in his cellars." It was a shot in the dark. Most clurichaun didn't want the people they stole from to know they were there. They could steal as long as the owner was completely unaware. Otherwise, they'd be run from the homes faster than they could pack up their things.

The clurichaun stomped back to her cracked doorway and thrust a bottle of wine at her. "Fine. Take it. But this is a one-time deal, then we're paid up."

"A single bottle of wine for a year of silence? You'll have to do better than that." She took the offered beverage, though.

He grumbled, counted on his fingers, then stuck out his tongue. "Fine. A couple a week?"

"How many is a couple?"

"Two."

"Three."

The clurichaun shook his head. "Two."

"Three, and that's the final offer."

His lip curled in a snarl. "You drive a hard bargain, faerie woman."

"Don't I know it." She held out her hand for him to shake, holding it in the air for a few heartbeats before he reluctantly shook it. "You've found yourself a partner, clurichaun. Pleasure doing business."

"Wish I could say the same." He waddled away from her, a bottle less in his arms, and she shut the door.

Elva pressed her back against it and stared up at the ceiling. What was she doing here? Drinking bottles of wine, soon to be buried under warm furs, for what? Why had he summoned her here?

She popped the cork and made her way to the bed. Her clothes remained on for the night. With the semi-transparent walls, the last thing she needed was the clurichaun getting any ideas. Or the bear.

Shivering, she sipped from the wine bottle and watched the walls for any shadows moving by. What could a bear possibly want from a faerie?

The question would plague her until she found an answer.

6

She was *here*. In the castle. With him.

No woman in her right mind would have traveled that far to trap themselves in a castle with a bear. It wasn't possible she was simply kind enough to…what? Blindly throw herself into his arms because he'd asked for it?

Donnacha shook his head, pacing the halls outside his own bedroom. The huffing growls of his breath bounced off the ice.

It wasn't possible that she'd decided to help him out of her own free will or the goodness of her heart. Just look at the woman. She was strong, powerful, and the sword at her side had the marks of use. He'd seen her use it on that strawman. Beheaded.

He might have grinned if it wouldn't have looked like a snarl. The woman would use that sword on whoever stood in her way, he was certain of it. Who knew women like that were bred in the Seelie Courts? He'd thought only dwarven women had that kind of fire in their chests.

But he was getting distracted. She was here, and that was going to cause problems for him.

The Troll Queen had thought she would be a diversion, clearly.

While Donnacha hadn't been thinking straight in the moments, or days, after she'd told him how to break the curse, he was now. The only reason she'd brought a woman to the castle was because she thought it would push him toward her troll daughter.

He couldn't figure out *why* she thought that. Bring a pretty little faerie woman into the castle? That was highly unlikely to make him think the troll daughter was a better option.

Of course, the dwarves and Tuatha de Danann weren't exactly friends. Although his cousin, Angus, had entertained a few of the tall, lithe creatures before, Donnacha was more in line with the rest of his family. Some of their faerie kin were good folk. Others, the Tuatha de Danann included, were not.

Having her here would be an unnecessary nuisance, but one he could avoid. He'd placed her in the fairest room. They wouldn't see each other often enough for either to form opinions. All he had to do was last for a year without her seeing his human face. That was a rather easy thing to do considering he was living as a bear. Nor did he have any portraits of himself here.

So, unless the Troll Queen had planned some nefarious deeds, he should be fine. One year wasn't that long to stay out of trouble.

Almost on cue, he heard the whispering voice of the Troll Queen. "Donnacha," she called out, her voice slithering through the halls. "Come to me."

He didn't want to. He should have known she would have something up her sleeve. Staying put would have been the smarter option. He could fight against the pull of the curse, and maybe she would give up.

His feet moved of their own accord. Donnacha padded toward the room with the mirror and slipped through the double doors.

She was already waiting for him. Her slate gray skin blended into the misty background of her home. Dark stone, dark shadows. There was nothing in the troll kingdom other than bleak, grim frost.

The Troll Queen stared at him, her face twisted with anger. "So, she made it to the castle."

"She did." He tried so hard not to gloat, but the faerie woman had done what no one else had ever managed to do. She'd beaten the Troll Queen at her own game.

"Well, that's a shame for her."

Donnacha locked his muscles tight, refusing to move when he realized the Troll Queen had, yet again, proven herself to be far more intelligent than he thought.

The creature in front of him laughed. "Did you really think that was the end of this, Donnacha? I plan to torture you until you agree to marry my daughter. You knew that the moment you chose to be cursed instead."

"She has nothing to do with this." Would the Troll Queen punish this woman as well? He couldn't have that hanging over his head. She was an innocent.

"She has a huge part in this. Because she's pretty, isn't she?"

Was this some kind of retribution for having a daughter who was ugly? Donnacha shook his large head. "You know my refusal to marry your daughter had little to do with her looks."

"It has everything to do with her looks," the Troll Queen hissed. "And now, I'm going to torment you."

He had no idea what she could possibly plan that would torment him further. Donnacha was already a bear. Already stolen away from his family. This knowledge made him more daring than he might have been otherwise. He tilted his head back and laughed. "Do your worst, Troll Queen. I will never give in to you."

She watched him laugh with a cold expression. "Donnacha, I know you better than you know yourself. You don't want to hurt anyone. You've never wanted to be the one who caused another person pain."

"The woman is off limits. You cannot hurt her."

"*I* don't intend to." She pressed a hand against her chest and smiled a feral smile. "You're going to."

His blood ran cold. "You can't force me to harm someone. That is also against the deal. You have no control over my decisions."

"I do a bit. But don't worry your furry little head. I'm not going to make you eat her, if that's what you think." She leaned closer to the glass and drew a long nail down the surface. The screeching sound was almost as terrible as her voice. "I'm changing the curse. Adding another layer to it, just a bit."

"What more could you do?"

"Every night, Donnacha of the dwarven clans, you will change back from a bear into a man."

He waited for her to clarify, only to realize that was her addition. That was it. He could finally be a man again? After all this time?

As he opened his mouth to speak, she lifted a hand. "Not so fast, dwarf. If this woman sees your human face, then you will have to marry my daughter."

Well, that would certainly make things more difficult. But it was nothing he couldn't overcome. He'd simply stay away from her at night. He'd lock her in the room to be certain she wouldn't wander and see him by accident.

It was a difficult way to live for a year, but it wouldn't be the hardest year he'd survived. Donnacha nodded firmly. "So be it."

The Troll Queen's eyes lit up with anticipation. "Oh, and one last thing. You have to stay in the same room with her while you're a human. Sleep by her side, in the same bed, for the rest of the time she's here."

"What?" he blurted. "Why would you insist on that? She doesn't know who I am!"

"No, she doesn't. Which means she'll be all the more likely to try and find out who you are. Remember, all she has to do is see your face. The moonlight. A flicker of a candle. There's so many ways she can see who you really are, Donnacha."

His mind whirled, trying to find the loopholes, and each one the Troll Queen struck down.

"You can't cover your face intentionally. No masks, no hoods. Just you, as you are. No, you cannot sleep at the foot of her bed or blindfold her either. You can't tell her anything at all other than you must stay with her, in her room, in her bed, at her side." The Troll Queen clapped gleefully. "Now *that* will be real entertainment. I'll have you in my castle anytime now. What color would you like the bouquets to be?"

"You have not bested me yet."

"Oh, but I will."

A shock struck him in the base of the neck. At first, he thought it was nothing more than a knot in his fur. They were sometimes pesky enough to cause actual pain. But then the electricity traveled down his neck and through his spine. He had a moment to grumble out a barely there, "What," before it burst into excruciating pain. The air in his lungs stuck in his throat, the sounds he wanted to scream already silencing themselves before he gave them life. His body crumpled to the ground. Paws curling in toward his chest, he shivered in pain. His jaw gaped open as he tried to curse her, to tell her she would never win as long as he was alive.

The Troll Queen smiled down at him through the protection of her mirror. "I forgot to tell you that it will be the worst pain you've ever felt in your short life."

The mirror went dark as he was swallowed whole by his own body. Bones cracked, crunching inward over and over again as they realigned themselves to a much smaller form. Hair retracted, slithering back inside his body like there were snakes writhing under his skin. But worst of all were the talons that tore through his skin over and over again, trying to get rid of the muscles and fat that had built up in his bear body over the years. He leaked refuse and innards, coughing it up through his mouth.

Finally, it was over. He laid in a shivering mess on the floor. He drew his knees into his chest and tried to catch his breath. Donnacha couldn't even enjoy being himself again for the pain shook that through his body.

Every inch of his body was sensitive. If someone touched him, he might fly apart as his nerve endings screamed in agony.

The ice dug into his back. He was cold. So very very cold.

"Get up," he muttered. "Or it'll only get worse."

He knew the Troll Queen's game. She wanted to see him writhing on the ground in front of her. She wanted to know he was angry, that he hated being alive. That was the point to all of this.

And he refused to give her that satisfaction.

Donnacha rolled onto his side, then pushed himself to his feet. He held out a hand in front of him, staring at the half moons of his nails and the dark hair lightly dusting the backs of his fingers. He was a man again. Really a man.

He ran a hand down his chest, marveling at the way his ribs moved under his hand. His chest hair wasn't so thick that arrows couldn't penetrate it.

Could it be? Donnacha reached a shaking hand toward his face and touched the carefully groomed, close-cropped beard. So the Troll Queen hadn't taken the only thing that was the pride and joy of the dwarves after all.

He desperately wanted to look at himself, to see the body that had been taken from him. But he couldn't stand to be in the same mirror's reflection where *she* had stood.

Dropping his hand, he forced himself to leave the mirror room and return to his own quarters. There was clothing there for him, the ones he'd kept just in case because he refused to give up hope that someday he'd be himself again. Curses were created to be broken, and he was going to break this one with the help of that faerie woman he'd placed in that room alone.

He dragged a sleep shirt over his head and then quickly tied on breeches. He wouldn't have normally slept in them but…well. She didn't seem like the kind of woman who would hesitate to geld a man slipping into bed with her.

The curse tightened around his neck, urging him to hurry or else. The pull at his belly was directing him toward the Troll Kingdom. If he didn't rush to that faerie woman's room, he'd find himself running through the halls of the Troll Queen's palace, hoping he could get away from that monstrous daughter of hers.

He stuffed the loose ends of his shirt into the pants and then ran down the halls. Slipping and sliding, he slammed into a few walls before he finally resorted to skidding down them. He remembered how slippery the ice was without claws.

No claws were on his feet to help him move, he realized with complete and utter joy. The bare feet of a man could easily grow cold touching the smooth floors. It didn't matter at all. He welcomed the pain because it meant he really was in this form. He really *was* a man, after all this time.

Donnacha paused in front of the door to the faerie woman's room, wondering how he was going to do this. He couldn't share this joy with her. She didn't know he was the bear. She *couldn't* know he was the bear or she would pressure him to tell her what was going on.

She was already too curious about these circumstances, although he attributed that to Scáthach. The wily woman would be the kind to plant someone in his house just to make sure he wasn't dangerous. And he wasn't.

He was just a dwarf. Just a *dwarf* who could finally be the person he had been all those years ago. Even if it was only in the darkness where she couldn't see his face.

Donnacha waited until the sun set completely and a cloud passed over the moonlight. Then he pressed a hand against the outside wall of her room. The castle would help him. Of everyone involved in the curse, it liked him the most.

He envisioned the walls becoming something more than just ice. He imagined them fracturing, breaking like glass tossed onto the floor. A labyrinth of fissures that would break the light between them, bouncing within it but never passing through.

The ice that had created her room thickened. The crackling sound of magic echoed through the hall and, soon, the ice couldn't be seen through at all. Even light was caught on the fractures within the walls.

Blowing out a breath, he looked around him. "Thank you."

A cold wind blew through the hall, gently touched his back, and then continued on. He didn't know what spirit or creature haunted this castle, but he knew it liked him. That was enough.

Donnacha opened the door and stepped into the darkness of her room.

It was so quiet inside the walls, he thought she wasn't there. Not even the sound of a person breathing could give him a way to pinpoint where she was. Of course, he was used to having the hearing of a bear.

Then, he heard the sound of a body shifting against fabric and felt every muscle in his body tighten. Gods, how long had it been since he enjoyed the company of a woman as a man? As nothing more than someone who wanted to give pleasure and receive it in return?

"Who goes there?" Her voice floated through the darkness.

"No one," he replied, stepping closer in the dim light.

"The master of this castle said no one else lived within these walls." Again, she shifted. Sitting up on the side of the bed perhaps? "I apologize if these are your quarters."

"They aren't." He stepped forward, his eyes adjusting to the darkness until he could see the shape of her moving. "Please, stay."

He could see the silhouette of her arm braced against the side of the bed. The muscular length of it was so graceful. A long curtain of hair fell in front, or perhaps behind, slowly shifting forward like the dress of a dancer as she moved.

Fortunately, she couldn't see in the dark like he could. Dwarves were born in dim light, they lived in the mines and, thus, their eyes saw more than the average person. Where she likely only saw darkness, he saw details as if a full moon shown upon them.

"I'm afraid that isn't a sufficient answer for me," she snarled.

The ringing of metal against metal was his only warning to flinch backward as she drew her sword. As it was, the point still rested against the base of his throat. Cold, it sank beneath his skin just enough for a bead of blood to well up and drip down the blade.

Her hand tightened on the leather grip. "Start talking."

"I'm not here to hurt you, merely to lay with you."

She choked out a laugh. "I can assure you that's not going to happen."

"Not like that!" Donnacha tried to stop his thoughts from running away from him. Laying with her would be...an experience he wasn't likely to forget ever. Shaking his head, he stepped back from the sword she kept raised in the air. "Look, I can't explain. It's part of the deal."

"What deal?"

"You staying here with the bear. I can't leave this room, and neither can you. I'm not asking for anything other than for you to share the bed with me. We can put up a blockade of pillows if that helps you to trust me—"

"Trust you?" she interrupted, her words sharp. "What reason do I have to trust you at all? You, who has appeared out of the shadows in my room, sneaking through the ice walls like a wraith here to kill me."

"I'm not here to hurt you." He raised his hands even though she couldn't see them.

"They all say that," she muttered, but lowered the sword.

"Who?"

"Men," she spat at him. "They say they don't want to hurt you, but then they do it anyway. It's not your fault that your sex only knows how to leave marks that bruise."

His heart caught in his throat. This woman had been hurt. He didn't know how or why, but he intended to find out someday. "Those are not men," he replied.

"Then, please, enlighten me to what they are. Explain it to me, so that I might understand what truly happened to *my body*."

"You misunderstand me." Donnacha shook his head. "If a person says they won't hurt you and then do, it makes them a monster, a beast in the night to be hunted with sword or bow. I hope you cut off the hands of anyone who touched you without permission. And if they still walk with such hands, then I ask you tell me where to find them, so I might gift them to you on a golden platter. But those are not men. Those are not people, only animals who deserve no better treatment."

She remained silent for a moment, her breathing ragged but her silhouette still as stone. Finally, she made a soft sound of disbelief. "Pretty words, stranger. Tis a shame they aren't anything more than poetry."

He watched her sheath the sword and settle back into the furs. Did that mean he was allowed to join her? He didn't want to end his life by enjoying only a few moments as a dwarf before a wounded woman put a blade through him.

But he also didn't want to push her too far. She deserved more than some strange man appearing in her room and forcing her to…what? To tolerate his company?

The Troll Queen was truly more vicious than he thought. She must have known this woman was a wounded soul. And what person would put another through something like this? To force this woman to endure his presence when she was clearly afraid, trying to protect herself. This was worse than he ever imagined the Troll Queen could do.

He sat at the foot of the bed, tilting his head to the side and watching her over his shoulder. "I wish I could leave you. It's not by choice that I am here, and I would have you know that if I did have a choice, I would bid you good night."

"I understand not having a choice, stranger. If you touch me, know that I will remove that hand."

"Understood." He smiled. She'd taken his advice to heart then. Good, it was the dwarven way to show man or woman what happened when they touched things that weren't theirs.

Silence fell in the room. It wouldn't be so bad to spend a night like this, he decided. The air was cold and his feet were already going numb, but he was still a dwarf. How could he sleep at a time like this? When he finally was himself again?

Donnacha flexed his toes and grinned. They moved like normal feet! Not pads or paws, but feet with toes and tiny toenails that he'd have to look at with light tomorrow night before he had to come back here. His arms and shoulders felt frosted to the touch, and a shiver shook through him.

A shiver.

When was the last time he'd even felt the cold? He couldn't remember. Only that he'd always felt so much more capable of handling it than now.

Furs fell over his shoulders and arms, two or three of them. He couldn't untangle the heavy masses to guess how many she'd chucked at his head.

"You'll keep me up with that infernal shivering," she snarled, pulling more of them over herself. "Stop it."

The grin on his face spread wider. "I can't help it if I'm cold."

"Then get out."

"Can't do that either." He folded the furs around himself more tightly, reveling in the feel of them against his fingertips. Had fur ever felt this soft? He could only remember it as a distant item in a life he'd thought long gone.

Warm, he crossed his legs and placed his hands on his knees. Perhaps in this form Donnacha could remember more of his life. He'd spend the night reliving what it meant to be human. Knowing what his family had felt like in the moments when they had sang into the darkest parts of the earth, coaxing gold from between the stones.

Just as his mind settled, he heard her quiet words.

"Did you mean what you said, earlier?"

"About the people who hurt you?"

She didn't reply, but she didn't need to. Donnacha knew what she was asking for. He didn't try to touch her, didn't move at all. Instead, he inhaled slow and deep. "Our parents forgot to teach us that monsters don't just live in darkness and under our beds," he said quietly. "Sometimes they live in the minds and hearts of people. Those are the dangerous ones. The real things we should fear."

The mattress beneath him trembled. "And if they say they love you?"

Gods, she made his heart hurt. "If they love you truly, they will love the waves and the calm seas. They will love the sunlight and the storms. A person who only loves parts of you doesn't love you at all. And if they could harm any inch of your body, then they didn't love the whole of you."

"That's what I thought," she murmured.

He listened to her shift, rolling over and turning her back to him. This strange woman was more than just a warrior sent to watch him. She was broken, fractured along the edges of who she should be. Just a bit, but more than any other warrior would have admitted.

Donnacha waited until her breathing evened out before he allowed himself to truly stare at her. To watch the outline of her ribs expand and the way her golden hair turned silver in the moonlight.

Who had hurt her? And why did that suddenly seem far more important than breaking any curse?

7

Elva held the blade over her head, muscles burning, lungs working in overdrive. It was a good kind of hurt. The kind of ache that meant she was alive, she was well, and that she was capable of fighting still.

She'd found the small garden hidden in the center of the castle. It wasn't much, just a natural hot spring and a small patch of green. But there wasn't any ice here, and that meant she could take off the straps of nails and actually walk as she was used to.

Of all the things to get on her nerves here, she hadn't expected it to be the cold.

Steam rose in the air from the spring. It coiled in lazy wisps that tangled around her legs when she got too close. The heat was welcome, the touch was…not.

She slashed down hard with the sword, battling an invisible enemy. The man who had appeared in her bedroom three nights in a row was bothering her. How could he not? His words were haunting in their effect.

Men should have their hands removed if they touched a woman unwillingly? Of course, she agreed. She'd wanted to chop off their heads as well, but how many people had admitted such a thing to her?

He had arrived each night nearly at the same time. And each night, he sat at the foot of her bed.

Elva knew he waited until he thought she was asleep to continue with his strange routine. At first, she'd thought he was there to haunt her as some kind of mythical creature who would crawl into her dreams and make her see things that weren't there. Or perhaps he was going to take advantage of her the moment she let her guard down.

He hadn't done either. Instead, he appeared to meditate. He crossed his legs, braced his elbows on his knees, and then…sat. For hours without moving. Almost like a statue or some kind of strange gargoyle who had decided she needed protecting.

She whirled, light bouncing off the blade as she dipped low and shoved the sword up. If there had been a person standing in front of her, she would have gutted them. A pity there wasn't. Elva could use a fight to blow off some of this steam.

She didn't understand the man who had made it quite clear he had no interest in bothering her. Yet, he was in her room every single night.

Was he really some kind of guard? The clurichaun had said she shouldn't leave her room at night. *Strange things*, the creature had said. What did that mean? Were there spirits who haunted the castle, or was it the bear she had to worry about?

Not that Elva was really all that worried about the furred creature. He hadn't appeared in quite some time. In fact, she hadn't seen him since the first day she'd arrived.

Yet another odd happening in this place. If he'd asked for her specifically, said she was the only one who had to travel to his castle, then why would he ignore her once she was there?

There were too many questions and not nearly enough answers. She didn't know which way was up anymore. But she'd be damned if she would wait much longer for an explanation. The next time she saw the bear, she was going to demand he give her… something. Anything.

Like he knew what she was thinking, the heavy sound of paws interrupted her thoughts. Elva blew a strand of hair out of her face and waited for the bear to arrive. He always seemed to know where she was in the castle. She didn't want to think about how that was possible.

As she swung the sword through the air, the bear padded into view. His nails clicked on the ice hallway that opened up to the small garden at the center of the castle. Then, she couldn't hear him walking at all.

For such a large beast, he was rather quiet. She wondered if that was how he'd managed to sneak up on Scáthach and her warrior women. Not a single one of them had realized he'd arrived until he was waltzing into their home like he owned the place.

Sweat trickled between her shoulder blades. "Haven't seen you in a while," she commented, holding her position until her arms burned.

"I've been busy."

"Doing what?" Elva carefully drew her sword down, the movement slow, no longer pretending to fight. Instead, this would build her arm strength for the time when she *did* have to fight. "If there's no one else in the castle, then I doubt you have many lordly things to do."

The bear chuffed out a breath and paused next to a blueberry bush that was, somehow, laden with berries. "Lordly? I'm not that."

"I didn't call you a lord. I said the things you'd have to do were lordly." A small grunt escaped her as her arms began to shake. "And considering you're not doing them…"

"You're rather prickly. You know that?"

Of course, she was. She had to be. After all the things Elva had gone through, all the people who had tried to take advantage of her… She couldn't count the reasons for her not to trust just anyone who walked into her life. There were too many of them.

She spun, whirling and tossing the sword from hand to hand. When she stopped, she lifted the blade above her head again and pointed it at him. "Give me a reason to not be prickly."

It almost seemed as though he smiled. "I have no interest in changing you, faerie woman. What did you say your name was again?'

He must be saying that to get a rise out of her, but damned if it didn't work. Sweaty, tired, and now growing angry, she let the blade drop. "You don't even remember my name?"

"I haven't had a reason to. Like you said, we haven't talked in a while."

"Elva," she snarled. "The woman who you insisted come to the castle and get stuck in this frigid place for some unnamed reason. Were you just lonely?"

When he shrugged, she grew even more infuriated. Did the creature not care that he'd ripped her out of her life? That he'd somehow managed to convince the most powerful warrior in the known world to just give her up like she was nothing, no more important than all the other women in the camp?

The sword shouldn't touch the ground. It wasn't *her* sword or even her weapon of choice, but Scáthach would have words for her if she didn't keep the blade well-oiled and sharp. Elva held it away from the ground and made her way to the small stone benched tucked into the bushes near him. She'd sharpen it, clean the whole thing if she had to, but she was getting answers out of this beast now.

"What's your name?" she asked.

"You may call me what I am."

"Bear?"

"It's as good a name as any."

Elva slumped onto the bench, reached underneath it for her

small pack, and rummaged through it for the oil and cloth she always carried. "It's a terrible name to call someone."

"Would you prefer to make up a name for me?'

"If that's what it takes." She looked him up and down. "You look like a...Liam maybe."

"Liam?" He huffed out a breath and laid down next to the bush. "Hardly."

"So you do have a name." Elva hadn't been wrong. There was more to this beast than simply the form he had taken.

She looked over the blade in her hands. She hadn't let it touch anything else, so it didn't necessarily need the oil. However, she preferred to make certain it was done right. If not for Scáthach, then for herself. The repetitive motion cleared her mind.

"I *had* a name. It's not one I use any longer."

"Why not?" she asked.

"There's no use for it when there's no one here to call me by name."

Elva grumbled, then poured oil onto the cloth in her hands. "Are you certain of that?"

The bear shifted. His head reared back, and he tilted it to the side, eyeing her. "Quite certain there is only me and you."

Oil slicked the blade of her sword. She scrubbed a particularly difficult tarnished spot, one that had been there since she'd had the blade but still annoyed her all the same. "And if I said I'd already met two other people who lived here? Besides yourself and now me."

"Two?" the bear repeated. "That's not possible."

Elva let the silence stretch between them. The bear was chuffing out heavy breaths, but she wanted to focus on the sword. Or at least, make him think she was focusing on the sword. Internally, she was trying to plan the right way to say the next words to him. She'd enjoyed the perks of having wine in her room every night since it made sleeping here a little easier and she didn't want to give up the clurichaun just yet.

"Why does it seem you're more surprised that there are two, and not that someone else lives here?" she asked quietly.

"I'm surprised someone has slipped under my nose."

She didn't think that was it at all. Staring at him, hoping she could see past the guard of fur and dark eyes, Elva shook her head. "No, I don't think it's that. You know there's a man appearing in my room every night, don't you?"

His jaw gaped open, revealing sharp, dagger-like fangs. The bear struggled with his words for a few moments before he hung his head. "I was aware."

"And you allowed it to continue? Or did you know it was going to happen before I was here and didn't think to warn me?"

"I had no idea...*he* would show up," the bear grumbled.

She arched a brow. "Then if you know of him, who is he?"

The bear shook himself. "He's a traveler, you could say. Someone who is now tied to the castle and cannot leave its grounds."

"A traveler," she repeated. Somehow, it didn't seem likely the man was anything of what the bear claimed him to be. He was far too...odd. Too different and far too talkative for him to be anything other than a faerie. She just didn't know what kind he was.

"Why are you asking?" the bear inquired. "It seems you have an interest in him."

"An interest in the man who arrives in my bedroom each night uninvited? Yes, I do. I'd like to know whether or not I need to slit his throat in his sleep."

"Has he fallen asleep? Seems unlike him."

She narrowed her eyes at the bear. "I don't need someone to be unaware to kill them."

It didn't escape her notice that the beast knew the man didn't sleep while he was in her room. How would the bear know that unless he was speaking with the human man? Or unless he was the man himself?

Curses didn't come and go like that. They couldn't be removed at will except by the original curse giver, and this certainly wasn't some kind of shapeshifter. He didn't have the acrid scent of magic that always followed shapeshifters. Instead, she could smell the musty wetness clinging to his fur. He smelled remarkably like a bear.

She'd have to sniff the man when he came into her bedroom next time. That should give her enough of a hint. Changing shapes couldn't hide that smell.

Again, he chuffed. He wasn't trying to catch his breath since he was lying down. He certainly didn't seem angered by anything she said, and he hadn't moved suddenly. She realized that must be the sound of the bear laughing.

He was laughing at her? Or with her? At the thought that she would kill someone who had wandered into her bedroom without permission?

She glared at him.

The bear shook his head at her and bared his teeth. "Rest easy, Elva of the fae. I know courage runs in your veins instead of blood and that you would roar at the sky if it offended you. I will not tempt your blade any more than I would set myself on fire."

"You?" she asked. "Or the man in my room?"

His gaze canted back to the ground.

"Ah," she said, looking back at her sword. "You can't speak about anything that pertains to your curse, can you?"

The bear did not reply.

"I'll say it now then. I think you are cursed by one of my own kind. I thought you were a human male at first, but now I think you're one of the many faerie species. And I think that you are the man who enters my room each night, although I cannot hazard a guess why the curse is lifted at night. Is any of that correct?"

He looked up at her then. "You know I can't answer."

There had to be a way around the curse. She'd never seen one before that didn't have loopholes, and she intended to find one in this. Elva thought for a few moments, then licked her lips. "Can you tell me the name of the man who shares my bed?"

For a moment, the bear looked like he wasn't going to respond to her. Then, he opened his mouth and said, "Donnacha." His eyes widened in shock.

"Even that has been taken from you, hasn't it?" she asked. "The ability to introduce yourself like a person."

"I am not the man who enters your room at night," he replied.

"No," she said with a grin, "you aren't."

She'd solved a portion of the dilemma. He couldn't talk about himself, but he could talk about the other version of himself, it seemed. That was a start. She'd have to ask the bear questions about the man and the man questions about the curse.

This was all rather convoluted.

Elva put her weight into cleaning the blade, trying to distract herself. There wasn't a reason for him to be cursed. Not that she had seen yet. This man was as complicated to understand as the curse that bound him, but he wasn't bad. In fact, she'd argue he might be the only good man she'd ever met.

No, that wouldn't do. She couldn't think like that when she'd been hurt so many times. He was going to do the same as everyone else did. Whether that was intentional or not, it didn't matter. Getting close to someone was just an excuse for them to hurt her when they left. And they always did.

She swallowed hard. How could she pull back from this? She shouldn't have smiled at him. He would take that as something it wasn't. As an admission he could get closer to her.

Would he use that in bed tonight? Would he try to slither closer to her? To tuck himself under the covers? Then she'd have to force him to move away. What if he didn't?

Her throat closed up at the mere thought. She knew how to protect herself in so many ways, but she'd never been able to stop *him* when she hadn't wanted to be touched, loved, even thought of. And that was partially her own fault. She'd never told Fionn to stop. She'd never told him she didn't want to sleep with him, she didn't want to marry him, and she wanted him to treat her better.

But how could she when her throat had closed up? He'd just wanted her to *love him*. He was the king of the Seelie court, why couldn't she love him?

The bear cleared his throat, the sound more growl than anything else. "You're doing that wrong."

She looked down at the blade in her lap. "Doing what wrong?"

"You're putting too much oil on it. You'll ruin the sharpness if you keep doing that."

What was he talking about? No matter how deeply she was lost in her own thoughts, she never made a mistake like that. Elva turned the blade over in her lap, then looked up at him with furrowed brows. "I was trained by the most talented of faerie swordsmiths. I'm not cleaning this blade wrong."

"And I—" He shook his head and corrected himself, "Donnacha was trained by the greatest dwarven swordsmiths. Trust me when I say you're doing that wrong."

She snorted. "Faerie swords are known throughout the land as the best swords ever made."

"And I think you'll find even the Fae admit that dwarves are better weaponsmiths." His eyes glittered with laughter. "As much as you like to argue, I don't think you can win that one."

Her jaw dropped open as she realized he was right. She couldn't argue with him about that because the dwarves were the ones who knew how to make the most impressive blades. On top of that, he'd managed to pull her out of a very dark train of thought. All without her realizing it until the anxiety in her mind loosened and she was back, sitting on a bench with a sword in her lap, looking at the bear who had laid his head on his paws and stared up at her with dark eyes.

"Just because I can't win that argument doesn't mean I'm not going to try," she grumbled.

"Argue away mistress of the fae. I like the sound of your voice."

He growled, showing his teeth in an exaggerated fashion that made her duck her head to hide a smile. "You get all snarly, like you're intimidating."

"I am intimidating."

"Oh, I don't know about that. I think you're a very brave woman, courageous even, but I don't think you're intimidating."

How many men had said that to her in her life? Elva was too pretty, too smart, too strong. Too much of so many things that it made people run. But it wasn't fair to complain about something like that when she had everything and nothing at all.

Elva bit her lip and looked back at the sword in her lap, tilting it enough so he could see it. "All right then. If you're such a scholar, what's the right way to clean this?"

8

Donnacha pressed his hand against her door, then leaned his forehead against the worn wood. He didn't want to go in there yet another night and force her to be in his presence.

She didn't want him there. That was clear as day. How many times were they going to have to do this?

A year. Three hundred and sixty five times was the deal, and each one was getting harder and harder to do.

He played back their conversation about swords and was startled to realize how much he liked her. At first, he'd thought she was nothing more than a simple warrior woman who had found her way to the Isle of Skye for revenge. There were plenty of women there for the same reason, so why should she be any different?

But then she'd figured out his curse. She'd realized a loophole even he hadn't thought to try, and she hadn't really even done anything. The way she spoke to him...

Donnacha sighed and backed away from the door. She'd talked to him like he was a man, not a bear. Like he was someone worth taking the time and effort to understand. To learn about who he was. Why he was kind, why he cared about what she thought.

Why he cared to help her clean a sword the right way.

He didn't have the answers to those questions. He wasn't even supposed to be talking with one of the Tuatha de Danann. The dwarves were a solitary folk. If he wasn't cursed, then he would have already been married to a cute little woman with a beard. They would have had children by now, a hole in the ground all for their own, and he'd likely be working in the mines during the day.

It would have been a quaint life, and it didn't include a tall, leggy, beautiful blonde.

She still hadn't explained who she was. Donnacha didn't blame her for that. He'd already guessed her story was one that would anger him. She was too beautiful to be ignored in the Seelie court, which meant he likely was going to want to kill the faeries even more than he already did.

Who would hurt her, anyway? He couldn't imagine someone wanting to harm her when the sunlight bounced off her hair like it was spun gold.

And it wasn't all about her looks, although he was dazzled by them often. She was such a fierce woman, more so even than the dwarves. Elva knew what she wanted and took it. But there was something else hidden in her that he tried to dig out. She was a question in his mind that he wanted an answer to. A brave, strange question that boiled down to why she was so standoffish but also so kind under that rough exterior.

The curse tightened at his stomach, pulling him toward a kingdom he wanted nothing to do with. He didn't want to end up in the troll kingdom. He didn't want to hurt Elva any more than he already had. It was a conundrum he knew would take a few more months at best to figure out, but that didn't make it any better.

Blowing out a breath, he pushed at the door.

She had gotten used to his visits each night. The castle had accommodated their needs, creating a small seating area in the corner made of ice. Elva had taken a few of the bed furs and created cushions for them to sit on.

As she had been for the past week, Elva was seated in one of the chairs. A small mound of snow sat between the two chairs where she'd placed an open bottle of wine.

Donnacha sank down in the ice seat beside her. "A rather cheery night for a drink."

She didn't look at him. Instead, she stared at the wall where the castle had opted to create a fireplace. The carved ice mimicking wavering flames was a nice added touched, although one he found slightly ironic.

He'd brought glasses a few nights ago, which she'd immediately tossed at the wall and shattered. They didn't need glasses because that was for civilized people, she'd claimed. Clearly neither of them was that. He had kidnapped a woman, and she had given up a life to be a warrior. Formalities were useless between the two of them.

Donnacha hadn't thought it was smart to argue when she'd been in a mood to break things. Tonight, she was silent.

He didn't know which was more frightening.

Reaching out, he grabbed the bottle of wine and took a sip. "Not much for talking tonight, is that it?"

"Old demons haunt me tonight." A rush of wind echoed her words, sounding like that of a spirit moaning through the halls.

"Ah. Anything I might help with?"

"Do you know how to banish memories for good? I'd wipe them from my mind if I could."

Oh, he didn't like the sound of that. Donnacha wasn't one for dwelling on dark topics, but those weren't words he wanted to hear her say again. "Banishing memories like that is a fool's errand."

"Is that so?" She looked over at him then, anger turning her blue eyes dark as a storm. "Do you have memories that plague you?"

He arched a brow. "What do you think?"

The knowledge of his curse dawned on her visibly. Elva shifted to stare back at the wall. "I supposed it's similar."

Donnacha leaned forward and braced his elbows on his knees, wine bottle hanging from his fingertips. "Those memories, however difficult they are to deal with, made you who you are. It's not a weakness to still be affected by them. You should be. They clearly were difficult times for you to endure, and you shouldn't be embarrassed by that."

What had he become? A sweet talker so that women would tell him their inner most secrets? His brothers would have laughed at him for saying something like that.

He'd realized a long time ago that memories were the only thing keeping people intact. They had to know what happened to them, to remember every harsh detail of life, to enjoy living. And for some strange reason, he wanted this woman to understand how important it was for her to acknowledge that.

Her face remained turned away from him. A muscle on her jaw jumped as she clenched her teeth, angrily staring at the wall. "I don't want to remember them."

"Sometimes it helps to share the memories."

"I don't want to tell you either."

"Why not?"

Elva's shoulders curved into her body. "I don't want to think about them at all. What makes you think I'd be interested in actually talking about it?"

He didn't think it would be a bad idea. In fact, considering the haunted expression on her face, it seemed like she needed to talk about it more than anything else.

He wasn't a qualified person to speak with her, certainly. She had no idea who he was. He had no idea who she was. There were a lot of factors that would make her not trust him.

Least of all that he'd forced her to come here. Elva had made it clear there was plenty she'd rather be doing than sitting in this fortress with him. She'd wanted to train, to become the most well-known warrior woman in the realm. Of course, she hadn't told him the why behind that either.

Donnacha thought he might be able to piece that together just from the way she was sitting right now.

His eyes danced over the signs of a person close to a breakdown. The way her fingers were curled into her fists. How she crossed her arms, nearly hugging herself, but still appearing sullen. And, of course, the way she was using her hair as a shield now. She didn't want him to look at her face, or her eyes, and he had a feeling he knew why.

Sighing, Donnacha held out the wine bottle for her to take. "Take a swig and talk."

She took the wine bottle and drank deeply. Wiping her lips, Elva shook her head and remained silent.

"You haven't talked to anyone about it before, have you?" he asked.

"Oh, I talked." The words were practically a snarl.

"And they didn't believe you." It wasn't a question. He didn't need to ask her to know why she didn't trust anyone to speak about her experience.

She looked at him then, her eyes dark and her mouth thin where she had pressed her lips together. "How do you know that?"

"My sister," he explained, gesturing with his hands. "We didn't have an easy childhood. Even though we are related to royalty, dwarves are different. We were just cousins of the nobles, which meant we were like everyone else. She wandered out of the mines when she was little, was caught by a few of the Seelie Court who thought it would be interesting to see if dwarven women were really female, or if we were all just male. It didn't end well for her, and some people didn't want to listen."

It took every fiber of his strength to tell the story without reacting. He wanted to curl his hands into fists and destroy the men who'd done it all over again. Hate had burned in his chest for the Seelie Court for so many years, he didn't know how to dull the aching rage.

"What did she do?" Elva asked, her voice barely audible. "To deal with the memories?"

He shrugged. "I think she's the strongest woman on the planet. She married, had four children, laughs and dances all the same. Like nothing happened. Sometimes I see the same shadows in her eyes when it comes back to her. When she leaves her house and when she wanders without her family beside her. But...she chose to not let it change who she was. And for the longest time, I couldn't understand that kind of strength."

"Why?"

"I wanted to kill them." His hands shook. "I wanted to hunt them down and remove their heads from the bodies the moment she told me. But *she* was the one who said she didn't want that. Giving them any more time in her life was a waste, she told me."

Elva took another swig of the wine bottle. "I don't think I agree with her."

"Neither do I." He held out his hand for the bottle, suddenly needing his own encouragement. "So, are you gonna talk or what?"

She gave the bottle up easily enough. He knew she was staring because he could feel the heat of her gaze, the way she was desperately trying to distract herself from anything and everything in the moment.

Finally, she blew out a breath. "I am Elva of the Seelie Court."

He waited for her to embellish before he shook his head. "I knew that."

"Elva," she repeated herself slowly. "Of the Seelie Court?"

"Yeah, I got that part. Is that supposed to mean something to me?"

"How long have you been cursed?" Elva held up a hand. "Sorry. How long has it been since you've been involved in the court system?"

This question wasn't tied to his curse and, therefore, much easier to answer. Donnacha shrugged. "A couple years?"

"That's it?"

"It's felt like a long time," he muttered. He'd been a bear for years now. That had to count for something.

"You should have heard of me. Or of what happened. You know the Seelie King has been removed from his throne, don't you?"

"Yeah, and tossed into the human world. What of it?"

She squeezed herself tighter. "I was his wife."

His jaw fell open in horror. "You're who?" Oh, gods. He had the previous Seelie King's wife in his castle? Was that what the Troll Queen had wanted this entire time? She hadn't been kidding when she said the court system would likely kill him. They would want this woman back in their clutches as soon as possible. He was shocked they hadn't already come searching for her.

"I'M NOT part of the court system anymore if that's what you're worried about. Give me that." She swiped the wine and took a deep drink.

"So they aren't going to knock on the door of the castle, demanding I give you up or I will part with my head?" he asked. The clarification felt rather important in this moment, no matter that she wasn't worried.

He was.

Elva shook her head. "No. The current king and queen understand that I want to be left alone. I needed to find myself again."

"After being queen."

"I wasn't a queen," she corrected him, taking another swig of the bottle.

Enough of that. He didn't want her getting drunk and then forgetting she told him all this. Donnacha reached out for the bottle. "Pampered then? No wonder you're comfortable here."

"Oh, I've gotten enough of that in my life, thank you very much. I'll break the bottle over your head if you keep up with the sarcasm."

Donnacha wrangled the wine bottle from her hands. The woman would not drink away her issues on his watch, no matter how much she wanted to. He put it on the other side of him, far away from her hands, and then turned back to her. "So he was the one that…?"

"Not like you're thinking," she muttered. She tilted her body away from him, back to staring at the carved ice flames. "Look, when it all started, I was very much in love with him. Fionn was a good man. Charming, entertaining, he promised me a life that I had wanted since I was a child. It seemed like the best choice at the time."

"You loved him or you wanted what he could give you?"

She shrugged. "A little of both? He was the first man I was ever interested in. First love, I guess. He wanted the best for me, no matter if I wanted it or not. And that was when the problems started. I realized I didn't want all the pretty things, but he thought I had to have them. He wanted to put me on a pedestal and tell me what I wanted."

That explained why she was so independent. For a woman who had been essentially a queen, Elva was still very much a gritty warrior. He didn't know many women who could switch positions like that. He crossed his arms over his chest and leaned back against the arm of his chair, staring at her profile. "All right. So he wanted what was best for you. What's wrong with that?"

"He didn't listen to what I wanted. He told me what I should want because that's what everyone else wanted. Fionn was all smoke and mirrors when it boiled down to it. He didn't know who he was, what he wanted out of life, anything other than the throne. Even that he'd only taken because his twin had it first."

Donnacha had known men like that before. He wasn't particularly fond of them, but they seemed to do well in life. Their wives were always happy, but Elva wasn't the kind of woman to settle for mere happiness when bliss was just out of her reach.. "And?"

"And eventually I realized the man I was sleeping with had turned into someone else," she replied. She turned toward him, looking him dead in the eyes with a cold gaze. "I didn't tell him. Any of it. I didn't tell him that I'd fallen out of love or I didn't want him to touch me anymore. I endured. That's what women are supposed to do, aren't they? I endured for years."

"Until you couldn't take it anymore."

She shook her head, nothing but dull cold reflecting her eyes. "No. Someone else came into the castle. They took Fionn's place, destroyed his reign, and then gave me the option to either leave with my husband or stay."

"Ah," Donnacha replied. "And you chose to stay."

"I did."

"Hardest decision of your life?"

"No," she replied, and a shadow darkened her eyes. "The hardest decision was to not tell him that I wasn't going with him. I stood there and watched as he was banished. I knew he was still in love with me. He'd wrapped his world around me, and I wasn't going to leave with him. I carry that guilt with me every day. I told him nothing. I didn't tell him that every moment he touched me, every night we lay together, I felt as though he were ripping something out of me.

"I can't tell other women who have experienced this. He didn't *force* me to do anything. He didn't know he was doing anything wrong. And yet...it feels like he was doing something wrong."

Gods, what did he say to that? This woman was already so torn up about this and, honestly, there was nothing for him to say.

He was a man, just like the person who had hurt her. She clearly didn't want to trust him, and she shouldn't, not that easily. Instead, he blew out a breath and stared at the flames with her.

How did he make up for the actions of another person? He didn't. That was the long and short of it. Donnacha couldn't track down the Seelie King and force the man to apologize. He couldn't take away the memories because he stood by the words he'd said. They *had* made her into the woman she was right now.

She wasn't weak, although she likely didn't want to hear him say that. She wasn't some creature that no one could love because she'd made a few mistakes. He knew that for certain because he was exactly the same.

But she wasn't ready to hear any of that. She was still holding herself like she was going to fly apart if she didn't clutch her ribs.

Maybe she would. And it would be a good thing if she finally let go of all that guilt and let it pour out of her as tears.

Only when she was ready, though. He wasn't going to push her.

A telltale clanking echoed from the hall. Donnacha stood without looking at her, strode to the door, and opened it wide.

The red-headed faerie in his hall froze. The clurichaun clutched six bottles of wine in his small arms. His green eyes widened and his ruddy cheeks proved he'd already been drinking the day away.

"Donnacha," the clurichaun said.

"Give me three."

"Master, I don't think—"

"Three," he snarled.

The faerie handed them over awkwardly and then took off running down the hall. How he'd managed to sneak into this castle without the Troll Queen tossing him on his arse, Donnacha would likely never know. It didn't matter, though. The man had served his purpose.

He closed the door and brought the wine bottles with him back to the seating area. Elva stared at the wall, still lost in her own thoughts.

"Here," he muttered, popping the cork on one of the bottles and holding it out to her.

She took it, glancing at him in confusion. "Didn't you say I wasn't drinking anymore tonight?"

"Normally, I would say drinking your feelings away is a bad idea." He ended the words on a grunt as he popped a cork on another bottle for himself. "But tonight seems like a good night to share a drink with a friend."

She arched a brow. "Are we friends now?"

"Well, I'd like to think so." He leaned forward and clanked their bottles together. "We'll see by the end of the night. I don't associate myself with those who cannot hold their liquor."

Elva snorted. "You might be a dwarf, but I'm quite certain you haven't drank anything in at least a few years."

"Doesn't mean I can't drink you under the table, faerie. All your kind have a rather delicate constitution."

She rolled her eyes. "Try me, dwarf."

And so he did.

9

Elva's heartrate sped up, pounding in her chest and making her breathing difficult. The night was cold. Frigid even. She could see her breath in the air, and any part of her body that was exposed to the air felt like ice.

He still sat at the end of the bed, as he always did. It wasn't fair for him to stay there. She still didn't understand why he had to linger in her room, but apparently the topic was still off limits, whether he was talking about his bear self or the human man.

What kind of curse required him to stay in the same room as her? She had never seen his face at all. Just the dark outline of his body in the shadows. Even when they were drinking together, she could just barely see his movements. So what was the point of forcing him in here with her? To be so close to someone else, but never really within touch?

Elva stared at his silhouette. He wasn't likely to hurt her. Yes, he'd said over and over that he didn't want to touch her if she didn't want him to touch her. But everyone always said that.

She'd found even the most trustworthy of men could turn on a dime if they wanted something. It made it damned difficult to plan her life around them. He could just…decide he wasn't going to be so nice anymore.

"Why are you staring at me?" he muttered.

"I'm not."

"I can feel your eyes on me. Stop staring and go to sleep, Elva."

She pulled the furs up a little too roughly. "I'm not staring. And I can't sleep, so you can stop telling me what to do."

The blustering sigh he released was enough to let her know he didn't believe a word she said. "Elva."

"What?"

"You know what."

The man had gotten into her head more than anyone else had in a long time. Even Scáthach with all her talents and trustworthy nature hadn't gotten Elva to talk about her history. What was it about this man that made her want to open up? He wasn't safe to be around. He had been cursed, and in her experience, cursed men weren't that way because they were kind souls.

Of course, this could all be the anxiety talking. She could hardly be around men now without losing her breath. Even Bran, her dearest and oldest friend, made her want to vomit just by touching her.

This cursed dwarf didn't make her want to puke. In fact, he just made all the thoughts in her mind quiet.

Or most of the time. But not tonight.

She sighed and tucked her nose into the fur. Elva was a warrior. She had built a new life upon strength and capability. She didn't need someone else to give her a reason for loving the way she was. That was what she'd fought so hard for. This state of mind that allowed her to rely on herself rather than another person.

And yet…she wanted to rely on someone else. She was so damned tired of being alone all the time.

"It's too cold for you to be out of the covers," she finally said.

"And I'm not going to take the bed, nor do I see another bed in this room. I'm fine, Elva. I've experienced nights colder than this."

There he went, confusing her again. How many men would argue with her when offered a place in her bed? She didn't know of any man who would have. This dwarf didn't make sense, but he certainly made her feel more like herself.

Grumbling, she flipped the furs on the other side of the bed. "Just get under the covers, would you? I'm exhausted, and you're shaking the whole mattress with your shivering."

"I'm not shivering," he replied, laughter dancing in his words.

"Donnacha."

"Elva," he replied.

Then he moved. She held her breath as he crawled up the bed and underneath the covers. Would he try to touch her? Would he pull her into his arms? She didn't know if she could handle that. Not right now when her heart was thundering in her ears and her hands were already shaking.

She gripped the furs as tightly as possible, turning her face toward him and waiting for the moment when he would insist she use her body to pay for her stay here. That she was too pretty for him to resist. That she wouldn't mind, would she?

He didn't say any of these things. Instead, Donnacha sighed and stopped moving.

She waited a few more heartbeats before asking, "Warmer?"

"Much."

Silence fell between them, pressing down on her lungs until she forgot entirely how to breathe. He was *here*. So close she could touch him, and that was somehow more suffocating than if he had been sitting directly on her chest.

She wanted to run. She wanted to get up and bolt, but that wasn't normal behavior. The ghost of Fionn loomed over her. It whispered in her ear that she would never be a normal person after him. That she couldn't think like a normal person because she wasn't one anymore.

He'd sunk his claws so firmly into her that she'd never be able to look at a man the same again. She'd never be that innocent little thing who was so kind and forgiving. Elva would never be herself again.

Donnacha cursed and threw back the covers. "I'm not doing this."

"What? I already invited you to stay under the covers, Donnacha. Where are you going?"

"You don't want to do this," he growled. "I'm not going to make you uncomfortable just for a little frost. I'll be fine, faerie. Just—"

She reached out and grabbed his arm. All she could think was that he should stay. She could learn how to be a normal person without having a panic attack.

And then, all she could think was that he wasn't just a short little creature like most dwarves. He wasn't covered in fur like a bear pelt. His arm was warm, strong, muscled far more than she would have expected.

He felt like velvet under her hand. Not smooth like Fionn had been, like a sculpture or glass. But textured with hair, scars, and the feeling of another person. He was *real*.

"Stay," she repeated. "It's okay."

"You're the one shaking now," he said, remaining firmly at the edge of the bed. "And I don't think it's because of the cold."

It wasn't. And she was embarrassed he'd realized his closeness had affected her. "I can't let it run my life for any longer. The idea of being alone for the rest of my life terrifies me. But I can't even sit next to someone else, let alone sleep in the same bed."

"So you want to throw yourself into the most difficult part first? You have to be a little gentler with yourself, Elva."

"It's my choice," she spat the words. "I get to decide how to heal my own wounds and, right now, we're both cold. This castle is made out of ice. We have to warm up, and we can warm up on other sides of the bed. Without touching each other."

He sighed. "We were already doing that, and clearly it wasn't working for you."

It hadn't been, but now he knew where her mind was. He understood she was panicking just from him being close to her. Somehow, that made it feel a little bit better. She wasn't struggling alone anymore.

"Just try again," she finally said. "It's warmer with you in the bed anyway."

Donnacha hesitated for a few more moments before he slid back under the covers. He was careful to remain as far away from her as possible. "Dwarves are like furnaces, so I've been told."

"Oh, really?" She stared up at the ceiling, trying to calm her thundering heart. "Who told you that?"

"An old lover."

"Any more details than that?" She let out a chuckle. "That could have been anyone."

He muttered a single word, clearly trying to muffle the sound.

"What was that?" she asked, quite certain she'd heard the right thing and holding in laughter.

"A banshee."

"A *banshee*?" Elva burst into laughter at that. So she had heard him right. But who slept with banshees? No one wanted to be around the terrifying things. "They are the souls of the dead. You know that, right?"

"Doesn't mean they don't have needs," he grumbled.

"Needs? Like sucking out the souls of those they deem unworthy of an afterlife?"

He remained quiet for so long after that she thought perhaps she'd insulted him. Then he expelled a breath that sounded suspiciously like a laugh. "Well, she was good at sucking something."

"Oh, for gods—" Elva whipped one of the pillows at him, striking him hard in the face.

Now, a full belly laugh rumbled through his body. He tossed

the pillow back at her. "You walked into that one, faerie! Come on, now. What else were you expecting?"

"A little gentlemanly decorum perhaps?"

"I could say the same about the woman prying into a man's love life. I'm not exactly prolific in my philanderings, if you must know."

She shook her head and tugged the furs higher. "Oh really? I find that hard to believe. Even in the Seelie Court, we've heard how dwarves find lovemaking to be...quite an experience to enjoy."

"Ahh," he sighed. "So the faeries of the courts do remember their old friends."

"Old friends? Is that what you call them? Seems to me you'd want to be with someone younger, but for a man who enjoys the company of banshees, I suppose I shouldn't be surprised."

"You'll never let me live that down, will you?"

Elva shook her head. "Not likely."

They fell into a companionable silence. Elva tried to keep her mind in that lighthearted state of mind. She wanted to focus on the way he'd made her laugh and the sound of his own happiness.

He had a way of doing that to her, a way of breathing life into a situation that felt so dark she couldn't inhale.

Except, now he was right there. She could feel the blankets moving with a twitch of his foot. Even the sound of his breathing reminded her that someone was right there. So close she could have reached out and touched him.

Did she want to? Elva wasn't really sure. She didn't know if that would make this infinitely worse, and then she'd have to ask him to leave. Leaving the room wasn't possible, which meant she had even less control over this situation than she wanted to have.

There was that tight feeling in her chest again. She curled her fingers in the furs and forced herself to relax through the panic attack. He wasn't trying to touch her. He was just trying to get warm. She could be here, force herself to live through the horribleness, and it would be fine.

"How are we doing over there?" he asked.

"I'm okay."

He shifted, rolling over in the bed so his silhouette was turned toward her. "Okay, now I'm going to ask that again, and this time you're going to answer me truthfully. How are we doing over there?"

"*We* are doing fine," she repeated. Then muttered, "I am not at my best, however."

"That's what I thought." Donnacha shifted a bit away from her. "Better?"

She assessed the situation. Her chest was still tight, her breathing irregular, her mind incapable of focusing on anything but the way her hands were shaking. "Not really."

"I'll get out of bed."

"No!" she shouted the word, startling even herself. "I just... Can you maybe stay where you are and reach out your hand?"

Elva wished she could see his face. She was certain he was wrinkling his brow at her. He stopped breathing for a moment, then settled back on the bed. Slowly, he slid his hand under the furs toward her and stopped in the middle of the bed. "Like this?" he asked.

"Yes."

Why was she asking him to do this? She wasn't going to like touching him. She didn't even like that he was so close. Asking him to move closer seemed foolish. But she was so tired of holding all this anxiety inside her. She was so tired of being *afraid*.

Elva slid her own hand under the covers until she was close enough to touch him. Did she really want to do this? She wasn't sure. Would this change their relationship? Right now she was enjoying being somewhat close to a man with no expectations. She didn't want him to think she was romantically interested in him.

That was so much of a stretch for her. She didn't know *how* to be interested in someone again. Not after everything that had happened to her. She was better off alone.

Far away from any man of her own species. Far away from anyone who could hurt her.

Wasn't that her problem? She'd taken herself out of the world, forced herself so far away from everyone else that she was hardly living anymore. Elva wasn't even a person at this point. She was a ghost who remained in the shadows, mimicking what life was but never actually enjoying it.

Elva shifted her hand again so she could place her pinky over his. That was it. That was all she could do tonight, but it was something.

She blew out a long breath and focused on the feeling of his hand under hers. It was a strong hand, like his arm. It was more than just the smooth, pretty texture that had been Fionn's. The Seelie King had never touched a weapon in his life.

Donnacha's hand was covered with callouses and a few scars she could feel just from where she touched him. He had the hand of a swordsmith. The kind of hand that had gone through battles and come back out alive.

The kind of hand who could hurt.

She waited for the overwhelming rush of emotion that was certainly going to crash over her head. He could hurt her. He could at any point. Gods, he could waltz in here as a bear and tear her limb from limb.

The emotions never hit her. Instead, all she remembered were the times he could have hurt her and didn't. In the garden where she'd talked to him. Every night when he'd sat at the end of the bed in a way to give her privacy and space. How he always kept it dark in the room and never commented on her panic attacks other than to help her get through them.

Who was this man? Why was he so kind? So understanding of

everything she was going through, even though she couldn't voice her concerns?

Elva sighed again and shifted her hand fully over his. Donnacha flipped his own hand over and linked his fingers with hers.

"Still okay?" he asked.

"I think so." She closed her eyes and prayed he wouldn't ask her to explain this change. She didn't know what she was doing. There were no answers to her strange decision to touch him after two months in his presence.

Maybe this was her desperate call for help. Maybe she really wanted to be someone that others could trust, someone another could love. Or maybe she wanted a reason to run back to Scáthach and tell her he truly was a monster.

That he was dangerous. So she could come back here and destroy him with a sword just to rid herself of her confusing reactions to him.

Donnacha shifted again, then murmured, "Go to sleep, Elva."

"Good night, Donnacha."

"Don't overthink it," he said with a yawn. "It's just sharing a little heat."

But was it?

10

The mirror loomed above him. Magic reached out to him, tendrils of power that wanted to overwhelm and destroy.

Donnacha knelt on the floor in his bear form. He ground his teeth together and refused to look up at the Troll Queen pacing on her side of the magical creation. She'd summoned him only to say nothing. Instead, she paced.

He stared at the ground until he could take her incessant movement no longer. "What is it you want?"

The Troll Queen whirled. The charcoal color of her skin appeared duller in this light. Or perhaps she was ill. He hoped it was some kind of plague that could kill her kind. "Your little faerie seems to be doing quite well here."

He felt a swell of pride in his chest. "Yes, she's settled in just fine."

"Well, that's really a shame. That wasn't the point of her being here."

Donnacha knew better than to gloat. He knew better than to tempt fate by pushing the Troll Queen when she could easily snap. But he wanted to look in her eyes and see her reaction when he told her they were growing closer by the day. "We've become friends," he said. "Perhaps, in time, we can become even more."

The Troll Queen bared her teeth in disgust. "How dare you? This was a punishment. A temptation you were not supposed to enjoy."

"And yet, I have. I've enjoyed myself greatly."

He was surprised to realize how truthful the words were. He was shocked that he hadn't realized it until now, but he did very much enjoy being around her. Even the darker times, like the night when she had panicked having him so close in her bed.

A sound of pleasure rumbled in his chest whenever he thought of how he helped her, even in the small ways. Whether that was to teach her how to better clean her sword or how to handle her time with another person in her personal space, he'd made a change in her life.

Donnacha didn't know how to put it in words how that made him feel. He was thoroughly, wonderfully, excitedly part of her life as someone she would never forget now. He'd done something more than just exist in her world for a few moments.

Such as it was, he looked at these moments as a precious gift.

The Troll Queen's lip curled. "Well, isn't that lovely? The little cursed dwarf has found himself a friend."

"She's a wonderful person."

"Yes, yes, I'm certain she's a wonderful little thing. The Seelie King did find her entertaining for a time. I'm certain she's told you all about that."

Was she trying to get under his skin? Donnacha shook his head and met her gaze. "Of course, she has. Friends tell each other difficulties like that. Did you think her previous marriage would make me think any less of her? That she was some kind of castoff from another man? She's a person, regardless of her history."

The Troll Queen stepped away from him, fading into the shadows of the room beyond. "I don't care what you think of her,

Donnacha. I've already brought someone to talk sense into your little...plaything."

"Someone?" What did the witch have up her sleeve now? He didn't want to think what kind of creature she'd pulled out of the woodworks.

The Troll Queen was connected, he knew that very well. She had so many dark creatures at her beck and call, he didn't know what to expect. Was it going to be some duchess who owed her a favor? Someone else who had made a deal with the disgusting creature lurking in front of him?

The grin on the queen's face said otherwise.

She laughed, tilting her head back while the stick-like hanks of hair shifted around her face. "Don't look so frightened, my dear boy. I haven't brought out the ogres just yet."

"Who did you invite to the castle?"

"Oh, no one particularly terrifying. Just the woman from her past. The one who lives down at the base of the mountain with all her little...children." The Troll Queen waved a hand in the air. "You know, the one who likes to fight with sticks."

"Scáthach?" he asked. "You invited Scáthach here?"

"Well, not invited really. I just suggested she might need to check in on her little student. After all, your faerie girl hasn't sent any news back, and it has been months."

He frowned. Months? That wasn't possible. Perhaps a month, that he could believe, but so many months?

"You brought the castle into the faerie realm," he muttered, realization dawning on him. "The entire castle?"

"Oh, dear. Did I not tell you that? Your little faerie woman might be here for a year, but it's going to be much longer in the human realm." The Troll Queen shrugged again, her eyes glittering with happiness that he was upset. "I didn't think she'd mind, considering she's one of us."

"She has business in the human realm."

"All faeries do. That's the best part of our existence. Hopping into the human realm and meddling with their lives gives us purpose. But she can't ignore her duties for such a long time. Your faerie woman is needed in her homeland. Unless, of course, you'd rather I contact her family and let them know she'd like a visit?"

He shook his head. Of what he'd heard Elva say, she wouldn't like to see her family. They were the last people he needed to walk into this castle when she hardly trusted him.

Yet again, the Troll Queen had backed him into a corner he couldn't't' get out of. He couldn't deny Scáthach entrance into his home. She had a right to visit Elva when so much time had passed.

Donnacha didn't like it. There was a reason why the Troll Queen invited her in particular, but he couldn't figure out why. What was she planning?

Grumbling, he got up onto his feet. "Fine. She's welcome in my home."

"Only if I invite her," the Troll Queen reminded him.

"Of course, your majesty."

"Now, those are words I like to hear." She looked him up and down, then lifted a brow in question. "You aren't worried at all, are you?"

"Should I be?"

"Of course, you should. Scáthach would like nothing more than to see you dead. She'd have you removed from this castle faster than you could breathe."

He shrugged his massive shoulders. "She'd have to convince Elva first."

The queen pressed a hand against her chest and let out a long breath. "You trust her, don't you?"

Did he? Donnacha hadn't really thought about it so much. He'd simply been enjoying her company. And he *did* enjoy her company more than he'd enjoyed anyone else's in a very long time. She made him laugh and think about his life in a light he hadn't known possible. She was a good person; he knew that to his bones.

But did he trust her? Apparently so, because he found himself nodding. "I do."

The Troll Queen stared back at him, and if he'd thought she was capable of any kind emotion, he might have thought it was sadness in her gaze. "Oh, Donnacha. Haven't you learned you can't trust anyone yet?"

The mirror went dark.

What did she mean by that? Every time he spoke with her, it felt like he was presented with another puzzle that didn't make sense.

The Troll Queen clearly thought Scáthach would come here to make trouble. That was clear enough to him.

In his dealings with the warrior woman, he'd admit she hadn't seemed to like him very much. But that didn't mean she was dangerous or wanted to see him destroyed. In fact, now that his castle had disappeared from the Isle of Skye, she'd likely be more kind to him.

Unless the Troll Queen knew something he didn't know. A sick feeling swelled in his stomach, pressing the contents of his belly into his throat. What if he was missing something? What if this was all about to change, and he was going to lose something rather important to him?

Donnacha blustered down the hall toward the center of the castle where he knew he'd find her. Elva had taken to training every day in the only place where she could. Usually, he accompanied her to comment on her form.

She didn't like it when he pointed out that her training was lacking. Scáthach herself had trained Elva, but she was still just a human. Faeries were capable of so much more than humans.

He lumbered into the gardens, not stopping until he was directly in front of her.

Elva paused in the middle of her swing, the blade hovering but an inch from his nose. She'd been perfecting a rather difficult spin he'd taught her a few days ago. He'd only seen another faerie do it once, and even that was a man who had been training his entire life in the art of dance.

But she could do it even better than that man. Elva was the most capable woman he'd ever met in his life. He handed her a problem, and she fixed it. Simple as that. There was no arguing, no questioning; she just took an issue and ran with it.

The blade shook a moment and then dropped. "What are you doing here?" she snarled. "I could have run you through."

"You're far too careful for that."

"It's a new attack," she muttered, sliding the blade into the sheath at her hip. "You don't know I have enough control yet."

"You do." He didn't question that in the slightest. She wouldn't have even tried the new move if she hadn't thought she could control it. Donnacha watched her stare at him for a few moments before he sat on his hind quarters. "Besides, not much can hurt me."

She looked up and down his bear form before a small smile appeared on her lips. "Yes, well, I suppose you are right about that."

He wanted her to look at him like that every day. The mirth in her expression was enough to remind him that he'd done something good. He'd made her smile, and that lit up the entire castle with her happiness. Or maybe, it was just that it lit him up from the inside out.

"Listen," he said clearing his throat, "I've been informed we're accepting a visitor."

"Oh, really? I didn't think many people came to visit you."

"They aren't here for me." He watched her stride toward the bench where she placed the sword down. "They're here for you."

Elva froze, her hands outstretched and still touching the blade. "Who is it?"

"Scáthach."

"Ah." The stress eased from her shoulders immediately. She

stood straight and turned back to him, a smile safely on her lips. "Well, that's not so bad then."

"I just wanted to let you know that she was coming." He also wanted to tell her to beware. Something was happening that he couldn't understand, and she needed to be wary for something that might tear them apart.

But he couldn't say that. First, because the curse would never let a single word cross his tongue. And second, because they weren't at that place yet. She would think him crazy for ordering her around. And he'd think he was crazy for trying to influence her decisions. Then, everything would be shattered because he didn't trust her enough to let her make her own choices.

Donnacha tried to smile through the snarl on his face. "Good. Then you'll be expecting her."

"Is she staying long?"

"The castle won't let her." It likely wouldn't even let her through the front door, but that was something he'd have to fix.

Unless...

Footsteps echoed on the ice behind him, crunching as only a human's feet could do. Scáthach's voice interrupted them, strong and powerful like a sword slicing through the air. "I believe the castle welcomed me in just fine."

He looked over his shoulder with equal parts anticipation and dread. "Scáthach. I had a feeling you'd be joining us today."

"Considering you've kept her away for months, I think it's only my right."

What right did she have to Elva? He wanted to remind her that she'd thrown this woman away to the bears. Quite literally. She had no claim on Elva or Elva's life.

Then again, neither did he.

Donnacha wanted to stay. He wanted to be part of this conversation, if only to defend himself because Scáthach certainly had nothing good to say about him.

He could see the anger in her gaze. The way she watched her

pupil with calculating eyes. Clearly, she had words to say to Elva and he wouldn't like a single one.

But it wasn't his place. He didn't have any right to guide Elva's thoughts in one direction or another.

Donnacha took a step back and bowed his head. "I'll leave you ladies to it."

"Thank you," Scáthach called out.

"You have until the sun sets," he replied, trying his best not to growl the words. "Then she's mine."

11

Elva watched the bear leave, brows furrowed in confusion. Why was he letting Scáthach stay here?

He had made it very clear he wasn't interested in having anyone remain in his homeland. Not without his permission and most definitely not if he didn't trust them. So why was he letting the most fabled female warrior of all time linger? Without anyone to watch over her?

Scáthach meandered away from Elva's side, looking up at the icy towers around them. "So, this is where the fabled cursed bear lives."

For all that Elva had learned in the human realm, Scáthach was still the woman who had pulled her out of a very difficult time. Elva respected the woman more than she respected her own mother.

She cleared her throat and made certain the sword at her hip was secured before answering. "It is."

"Not what I thought it would look like."

"Really?" Elva tried to remember the theories about this place. Had people said it was filled with monsters? She couldn't really remember. There was something dangerous about the bear, she remembered that part. But she hadn't ever heard what people thought his home looked like.

"I've always thought it would be a little more masculine. Not quite so..." Scáthach reached out and touched a hand to the ice of the tower. It came away slick. "Feminine."

Elva had never thought of it that way before, but her mentor was right. This place *was* decidedly feminine. A man wouldn't have chosen to live in ice carved so delicately that it looked like a piece of art every way a person turned.

Was this another clue? Could she use this to guess who had cursed Donnacha?

She nodded. "I haven't thought of it like that, but you're right. This place doesn't appear to have been built by a man."

Her mentor turned and cast a disapproving look at her. "You're supposed to be considering all the options here, Elva. That's why I sent you all this way."

She was supposed to, yes. Of course, she remembered her purpose. It was just...difficult when there was so much else happening.

Her nights were filled with *him,* the man who had somehow been hidden beneath the fur and mass of a bear. The mystery of this place was connected to him, she was certain of it, as well as the story of the bear and perceived threat to Scáthach's people.

They weren't her people, Elva realized. How could she feel a connection to people who were so angry? Scáthach had amassed all the angry women in the world and collected them in one place, only to send them off on their own lives once she was done with them. That wasn't a clan. It wasn't a group of family or sisters. It was just angry women, hoping to save their souls by learning how to punish those who had hurt them.

Maybe Donnacha was right. Maybe violence wasn't the only way to fix the way she felt.

Scáthach watched her with a calculating gaze. "Come, child. Sit with me and tell me everything."

She followed her mentor to the bench and sat down next to the woman. For all that she was a dangerous person, Elva still believed the fabled warrior meant well. Scáthach wasn't the kind of woman trying to make an army of others. She wasn't leading these women down the wrong path knowingly.

In the end, Scáthach was human. She didn't have the centuries of life Elva did, nor did she have immortality on her shoulders. Death would come for her as it had come for all others in her lineage.

Perhaps death was what made humans so blind to the rest of the world. They focused on themselves entirely, making their life happy for themselves because there was always the inevitable that they wouldn't have much time left.

Elva blew out a breath and expelled the story in the next. She held nothing back. Every detail of this place, Donnacha, the man and the bear, all of it until her lungs deflated and her throat ached from the words.

After it was done, she felt a little bit like a rag that had been wrung out of water. Tired. So very very tired.

Scáthach ran a hand through her hair. "That is a grievous tale indeed. Not the one I thought you were going to say."

"Really?" Elva asked. "Can I know what you thought was happening on this mountain?"

"I rather thought it was someone from my past coming to haunt me." Scáthach gave her a sheepish grin. "I'm ever so glad to see it's not, but I do apologize I brought you into this."

"That's all right."

"Now, we need to figure out how to help this man."

She couldn't have startled Elva more if she had said they should tear the castle to the ground. "What?" Elva bit the inside of her lip. "What do you mean?"

"I'm not heartless, Elva. I do not trust men, nor do I think they are a kind lot, but I don't like to see people who are suffering. This is injustice. No one should have to suffer through a life of a curse."

Gods, she agreed. Thank every ancestor that Scáthach saw this situation the way Elva did. With the two of them thinking of a way to break this curse, she was confident there was a fix.

"What do you suggest?" Elva asked.

"You said you've never seen the man's face, but you've seen the bear quite often?"

Elva nodded.

"Then there's some connection there. He claims you aren't supposed to see his face, but maybe, just maybe, you're supposed to."

That didn't seem like a faerie curse. Elva wanted to tell her that, but there was more wisdom in this human woman than most. She gestured for Scáthach to continue.

"I have a candle in my bag. I've used it most nights to note my journey here through the mists into the realm where both humans and faeries can exist. However, I will give it to you. Light it when he falls asleep and look upon his face. Perhaps that will break the curse."

"Or make it worse."

"Sitting and doing nothing is certainly making it worse already," Scáthach replied. She reached into her bag and brought out the nub of wax and wick.

Elva took it with more than a little trepidation. Would this be going against everything he'd asked of her? Although, he hadn't really asked for anything as of yet.

Donnacha had been a perfect gentleman while sharing her space. He'd taken the time to make sure she was comfortable with him being there, to explain he couldn't change it and wouldn't have imposed if it had been his choice.

But he'd never said she couldn't look at him. He'd never said she couldn't take matters into her own hands and… what? Violate his privacy in this way?

Would that make her the biggest hypocrite?

Scáthach reached out and covered Elva's hand, curling both

their fingers around the candle. "I don't know if it's the right thing to do. This is a choice you will have to make, as you've been here and I haven't. I will say *I* think it's the right thing to do. If I were here, I'd want to do everything in my power to break his curse."

"What if it makes everything worse?"

"Isn't it better to try something than nothing at all?"

And therein lay the answer to a question that had been sitting at the back of Elva's mind. She was a woman of action. She wanted to help, but doing nothing as he expected… It wasn't going to work for her.

Scáthach was right. They had to do something, try something, because she wasn't happy with him suffering like this. A bear during the day, and a man hiding in the shadows at night? That wasn't a life worth living. She refused to stand by and allow him to suffer like this anymore.

It was time to take things into her own hands.

Elva nodded firmly. "I will do what I must. First, I will ask him if I might see his face, though."

"That's fine. It's a good first step, and if he says nothing?"

"Then I will light the candle that night."

Was this the right choice? She wouldn't know until she took the leap, but it still felt wrong.

Scáthach stood up. "Come then, see me out of the castle."

"You're leaving? Already?" Elva stood as well, not sure how she felt about her greatest mentor leaving. It had been a relief to have Scáthach there.

Perhaps that was just her need for a mother showing its ugly head. Scáthach always made her feel as though someone had wrapped a warm blanket around her shoulders. The warrior woman took control of every situation she strode into. It was her way.

Now, Elva would return to a life where she had to do something, anything, but unfortunately all the choices were her own. No one else would be helping guide her in the right direction.

"Yes," Scáthach replied with a chuckle. "There are many who still need my training. But you?" She reached forward and took Elva's face in her hands. "You are so much stronger than the rest of them. I've always known that."

"I didn't show up strong."

"No one does. You all arrive at my door broken with your hearts hanging from your chests. I know what it feels like to have a man betray you. To rip out everything you were and are." Scáthach leaned forward and pressed her forehead against Elva's. "You have become something so much more than the pretty little faerie who walked all the way to the Isle of Skye."

Elva hoped the warrior woman was right.

12

Something had changed, and he didn't know what it was. Donnacha stepped into the darkness of her bedroom and felt as though he'd walked into a warzone. She wasn't seated in the chairs as they usually did before she grew tired enough for sleep.

Instead, Elva was already sitting on her side of the bed, staring at something in her hands. The light was too dim for him to make out what it was.

"Everything all right?" he asked.

She flinched at the sound of his voice, then tilted her head toward him. "I didn't think you would be here so soon."

He hadn't either. The change from bear to man had happened quicker than usual tonight. He didn't want to think about what that meant. The Troll Queen had something up her sleeve, as usual. It was torture to try to figure out what she had planned. Thus, he didn't even try.

Donnacha strode toward her. "How was your visit?"

He didn't like that Scáthach had been here, but it wasn't his right to say she couldn't visit her protégé. Elva had spoken of the woman like some kind of goddess. She'd said Scáthach had given her everything she had needed to become something more than the fragile faerie woman she'd always been.

Fragile? Donnacha had nearly burst into laughter when she'd said the words. He highly doubted she was ever a fragile woman.

Even now, he could easily picture her as she used to be. A golden flower in the middle of a field. A symbol of what a woman could become once they were sure of their strength, a woman to be reckoned with.

He'd met her kind before, the Seelie women who were so beautiful they were intimidating. As a boy, he'd wanted nothing more than to see them just a few more times, to catch a lock of their golden hair so he could remember the vision as they strode past.

Of course, the faeries had never let him close enough to do that. But he'd stolen a lock of *her* hair while she slept.

Was it unfair that he'd stolen from her? Perhaps. But the strand had been cast aside as if she didn't know how lovely she was. Someone should keep it.

He'd wound it around his thumb and wore it as a ring. She hadn't noticed it yet, likely wouldn't, considering she couldn't see him in the dark. It was better that way. Elva would easily realize he was growing far too attached to her.

Donnacha couldn't explain the feelings in his chest as he knelt in front of her. She was more than just a woman. More than just a faerie who had strode into his home, threatening his way of life.

She was strong, capable, and so unsure of herself that it made his heart break. She didn't see herself the way he saw her. She didn't see the way her inner light lit up the world wherever she walked.

"Elva," he said quietly, swallowing hard. "Are you all right?"

He didn't want everything to change just because Scáthach had been here. He knew it might. The warrior woman had a hold over her charges like a queen in her kingdom.

He had just hoped it wouldn't change so much that she wouldn't even talk to him.

Donnacha sighed, then stood. He wasn't going to change her mind by kneeling at her feet like a supplicant at prayer. No matter how much he would have sang the hymns for her happiness.

Rounding the bed felt a little bit like going to his grave, and pulling back the covers and getting in felt like burying himself. He'd known this would happen. Few women could remain interested in someone who was a bear during the day. The hope that had bloomed in his chest was a fool's errand. How could he not be disappointed?

The furs on the other side of the bed shifted as she joined him in the warmth. He flipped onto his back but hesitated a moment. Staring down at the shadows of his hands, he wondered what he could have done differently.

Should he have not let Scáthach in? That would have only made her hate him. She wasn't a prisoner here, damn it.

He tugged the furs up to his bare shoulders, perhaps a little too harshly. She'd know now he was upset, and the last thing he wanted was to make things more difficult for her. Scáthach had helped shape her into the person he so admired. That had to mean something.

Was this jealousy? Donnacha forced his hand to remain still under the furs even though he wanted to scrub his face vigorously. He had no right to feel jealous over someone from her past. Hell, she was older than he was in faerie years. She'd done more in that time, and more people, than he could imagine. After all, faeries weren't chaste like humans.

Jealousy had no place in their relationship. He'd run her out of the castle with that thought process. But the mere idea of someone else touching her, someone else having her respect and trust... It cut him to the bone.

"Donnacha?" Her voice floated out of the darkness.

"Yes?"

"Don't move."

"Okay." He hoped his voice didn't show how much his heart had lifted at her mere words.

Elva shifted in the bed, drawing closer to him. He had thought she wanted to hold his hand again. That had been *nice*. It was the only way he could think to describe it. Nice because it made his lungs cease to breath, his stomach tie in knots, and his throat close up because he had been the one to help her get to that point.

He'd helped. All he wanted to do with anyone was to help.

She slid closer, and then he felt heat blanket his side. It wasn't much really, just a woman resting her head on his shoulder. But gods, it felt like he'd moved the earth.

Donnacha remained as still as he could. Her body was stiff as a board against his, but that was all right. She could warm up to him slowly; he wouldn't rush her.

Finally, he felt a warm exhale against his neck. "You're very short."

He huffed out a laugh. "Well, I am a dwarf."

"I expected you to be…"

"Like a faerie?" He shrugged. "Not quite. Does that make a difference?"

Donnacha lost his breath when her hand came up to hesitantly rest on his chest. "No, I don't think it does."

Stay still, he told himself. *Don't touch her*. Because this wasn't about him. This was about her taking back her independence, choosing to touch another person and see how far she could push herself.

But then he might die if he didn't touch her.

"Donnacha?"

"Yes, Elva?"

Her head shifted on his chest, letting the full weight of her body fall against his heart. It was perfect. This moment when he finally had her in his arms, when she finally let go of her fear and trusted him not to hurt her, was perfect.

"Can you just…hold me?"

Could he? Donnacha had to tense his muscles so he didn't suddenly snap his arms around her so tight her back would creak. Carefully and, oh so slowly, he wrapped one of his arms around her.

His palm flat against her spine, just above the curve of her hip, felt as though he were touching divinity. She was so kind, so giving, and so unbearably strong to be doing this now when he knew what had happened to her.

If he sank into her heat a little more comfortably, it was because he didn't want her to think he was nervous. If he tilted his head a little bit to smell the wildflowers in her hair, it was only because he was trying to fall asleep.

These were the things Donnacha reminded himself as he drifted off. All was right in the world.

ELVA WAITED until she heard his breath even out before she let anxiety run her actions. She couldn't do this. She couldn't take this entire situation in her own hands just because she didn't truly trust him.

Who was this man? Was Scáthach right? Could she break the curse by looking at him?

She'd meant to ask him before he fell asleep, meant to whisper a question of whether it would work. But then she'd remembered he couldn't answer her even if she asked.

The warmth of his body eased her anxiety a little bit. It was worth taking the risk to help him. He felt…good. She couldn't remember the last time a man had felt good in her arms.

Then again, he was the first man to hold her in his arms and not want anything more than that. Elva had thought he would at least tug her closer, that he'd try to take charge of the situation somehow, but he hadn't. Instead, he's simply looped his arm around her like he'd done it a thousand times before and snuggled closer.

He didn't push. He didn't force her to do something she didn't want to do just to please him. Instead, he was there for her in quiet solitude.

Gods, this man was twisting up her insides. Suddenly, she questioned everything about men that she thought she'd understood. Had she been so wrong? Had she wasted so much time hating everyone and everything when *this man* had been out there?

She reached behind her for the wick of the candle she'd hidden in the furs. Her hands started to shake. All she had to do was one little spell, a candle lighting spell that every faerie knew since they were a child, and then voila.

Elva didn't like using magic. She'd always thought it felt a little unnatural when she could use her hands to do the same thing. Not to mention *he* had always wanted her to use magic. Over and over again until she was exhausted by the effort of it. Until she vowed to never use magic again because it still reeked of his lingering scent.

She wondered if Donnacha knew how to cast spells. Dwarves usually did, so he must be able to. Then he knew she could cast light whenever she wanted, and he'd always trusted her not to do this.

Or maybe it wasn't that big of a deal. Maybe he just preferred the darkness to the light.

Was he ugly? She doubted it, although his chest was covered in more hair than she was used to with faerie men. Still, ugliness was more about what was on the inside. Of all people, she should know that.

Just do it, she told herself. *Get it over with and then it's done.*

All it took was one little flex of power, and the candle was lit.

The flame danced in front of her eyes, merry that life had been given to it. A drop of wax heated, melted, then dripped down to touch her fingertip.

Looking down, she stared into the face of the man who had given her so much and who had no idea she was breaking the rules.

Donnacha was handsome, she realized breathlessly. Not in the way of faerie men, no dwarf could ever be beautiful like that. His attractiveness came from the depths of the earth as his kind always did. His cheekbones were the marbled cliffs of the mountains. His beard brown and warm as the earth. Long lashes fanned out over his cheeks and tumbling curls of dark locks spread across the pillow.

He was as stunning as he was hard. Strong as he was kind. A conundrum of a person and yet…perfect.

So damned perfect.

What was she doing? He was asleep, and she was gawking at him like a child. She shouldn't tell him she'd done this, whether the curse broke or not. Resolving to do just that, she leaned forward to blow out the candle, then watched in horror as a drop of wax fell from her fingertip and struck his collarbone.

He sucked in a breath, opened eyes so vividly blue it made her heart hurt, and met her gaze.

Would he be angry? Would he yell at her now when he never had before?

She prepared herself to hide the flinch, to retreat back into the cage of her mind.

But then, he smiled.

A great big smile that stretched across his features like the sun peeking over the horizon. He had crow's feet at the edges of his eyes and dimples on his cheeks. But it was the laughter bubbling in those blue depths that made her heart melt all over again.

He reached up in the golden candlelight and cupped her cheek.

"You're even more beautiful with these eyes," he whispered. "You're a walking heartbreak, you stunning woman."

She held her breath as he drew her down, his breath fanning across her lips. He inhaled deeply, his chest touching hers, but he didn't kiss her. Instead, he merely held her in place while he asked, "If this is a dream, then kiss me."

Oh, how Elva wanted this to be a dream. The sadness in his voice was almost more than she could bear.

She leaned forward before she could rethink her decision. Pressing her lips against his was the answer to a question she'd had for years.

Yes, his mouth seemed to say she could have him. She could have all of him without the guilt, without the fear, without the ghosts in her ears telling her she'd never be good enough. And, damned, if it didn't feel like he'd just healed a broken part of her soul.

His hands flexed against her back, then Donnacha pulled back enough to breathe. "This isn't a dream, is it?"

"No."

He stared into her eyes, smoothing aside a curl that had fallen in front of her face. "Listen to me, Elva. I need you to find me."

She furrowed her brows. Find him? He was right here in her arms, and she was quite certain she knew exactly where he was.

"East of the sun and west of the moon," he continued. "Remember that. Say it."

"East of the sun, west of the moon." It was an impossible place. There wasn't a way to get in those directions.

"Good," he said. "I'm so sorry you were pulled into this."

And then, he disappeared.

She only had a moment to realize before she hit the bed. "What?" she cried out before the floor tilted. The ice itself heaved and opened a tunnel where the wall had been. Had the castle entirely turned on its side?

She couldn't hold on and, with a scream, she slipped out of the bed, hit the ice, and slid down the tunnel.

Shards of ice tore at her skin and bedclothes. Elva covered her head with her arms, feeling them become slick with blood almost immediately as more and more shards sank into her flesh.

The wind blasted by her ears as she tumbled wildly from the castle, only to be tossed into the frigid air. She pinwheeled her arms, trying to turn her body before she struck, but to no avail.

Elva hit the snow hard, rolled through it, and settled in the cold. Breathing hard, she turned just in time to see the castle crumble. She did not have time to escape before the large chunks of ice and stone rained down upon her head.

13

Donnacha landed on his hands and knees. Hard stone met his body, sending a cracking pain to ricochet through joints. He'd be fine. They knew that or they wouldn't have summoned him so quickly, but that didn't mean he was happy about the treatment.

Her kiss still heated his lips. He wanted to touch them, but knew the Troll Queen would see the movement. Instead, he darted out his tongue to catch the lingering taste of her.

Ambrosia and caramel, he realized with a pleased grin. He'd never forget that was what she tasted like.

"Welcome, dwarf." The Troll Queen's voice boomed through what he assumed was her great hall. It wasn't much of one.

He looked up, casting his gaze over the gray stones and the dingy interior. It looked as though it had never been cleaned. Piles of refuse were heaped in the corners, food slopped on the floor, and dirt that had been tracked in from the outside smeared the stones with brown. Or perhaps it was blood. The trolls were a rather brutal race.

The Troll Queen sat with her daughter in twin thrones at the head of the room. She was as thin in person as he remembered her with a skeletal body that appeared to be made out of stone. Hard eyes stared at him in disgust. Long nails tapped against the arms of her throne as if he was the one wasting her time.

The daughter, however, was just as awful as he remembered. Where the mother was made of stone, her daughter was made of bark. The Troll Princess was a horrid creature, wrinkled and brown with knots of color along her skin, making her appear mottled. Tusks rose up from her bottom jaw to nearly touch her cheeks, above which beady eyes stared at him in hunger.

"The dwarf!" the Troll Princess exclaimed. "Mother, did you bring me the dwarf?"

"I did, my sweet." Her mother reached out to run a hand over her daughter's head, three clumps of thin hair sticking to her fingers. "Isn't he what you wanted?"

"He's perfect."

Donnacha tried to still the shiver that danced down his spine. He knew what the trolls wanted him for. They couldn't procreate with each other. Somewhere in the troll inbreeding, they'd managed to doom themselves. Or at least, that was what the rest of the faeries thought.

Unfortunately, this meant they were now kidnapping other faeries and forcing them to help bring children into the world. This was rather hard when the kidnapped individual was male, but he was certain they had ways of getting around that.

The sneer on his face likely gave away his thoughts. "Troll Queen," he muttered, getting up onto his feet and crossing his arms over his bare chest. "I'm afraid I don't know why you summoned me. There is still time in my curse."

A man had to try, didn't he?

The Troll Queen saw right through his words. She smiled, all sharp teeth and pride. "You've lost, dwarf. You can give up the bravado now."

"I haven't lost yet. She'll come for me."

The Troll Princess tilted her head to the side. "She? Mother? Who is she?"

"No one you need to worry about, my pet."

The look shot toward him might have lacerated his skin if the Queen had any magic left to her name. He knew transporting him from her magic-made castle would have depleted her of any power she had for a little while yet. He could toe the line if he wanted to.

Donnacha grinned and stepped closer, watching the Princess's eyes look him up and down as if he were something she wanted to feast upon. "*She* is a faerie princess who far outrivals you. The most beautiful woman to have ever walked this earth, and the strongest creature I've met in my life."

The Princess's eyes darted toward her mother. "What does this have to do with me having him?"

Before the Queen could reply, Donnacha interrupted. "Everything. It has *everything* to do with you and I, because I am well and truly hers already."

"Enough," the Troll Queen snapped. "You are no one's but mine. Wasn't that the deal we made? You could try to survive my curse, but if you didn't, then I own you body and soul."

"I didn't make that deal. No one made that deal but you."

The Troll Queen shrugged. "Semantics. I cursed you. That means we have a deal whether you wanted to agree to one or not. And now you're here."

"I won't marry your daughter under any circumstances."

"You don't have to marry her." The Troll Queen began to laugh, and her daughter joined in. The booming noises lifted to the ceiling with the last of his hopes. "My dear Donnacha, I don't want you anywhere near a throne. You aren't marrying her at all. You just have to...satisfy her. Long enough for an heir to be born."

Gods, he didn't want to think of that. No wedding, just a slave to a creature such as her.

There had to be a way to stall. A way around this so that Elva could get here.

Donnacha didn't doubt she would come for him. She was too strong to let someone take something from her this easily.

The Troll Kingdom was difficult to find, true, but she would manage. And when she arrived, he knew she would take action. In the meantime, he had to make certain he wasn't completely broken when she did get here.

Squaring his shoulders, he met the gaze of the Troll Princess. "You're happy with this arrangement?"

She nodded and wiggled her shoulders into the stone. For a second, he thought she was getting comfortable until he realized she was scratching her back.

He shook his head, telling himself to get through this. He could distract them, and he didn't intend on distracting them with his body. "Then you will forever be less important, less beautiful, and certainly less powerful than the woman who came before you."

That caught her attention. The Troll Princess sat up straight. "Why? I am clearly better than she could ever be."

Disgusting. He schooled his features into a smooth expression. "If you don't marry me, Troll Princess, then you will only have claim to my body. What you want a claim to is my heart, so that long after you are done with me, your mark will linger. So I will be yours forever."

"Forever is an awfully long time," she mused.

"Forever is a gift of immortality, and by denying that, you are forever making yourself second best."

Perhaps it was cruel to bait her such as this. She was, in mind at least, just a child. The Troll Queen had never allowed her daughter to live her life. The princess was sheltered, spoiled, and downright mean. He hated taking advantage of someone like this. It wasn't in his nature to use others.

And yet, Donnacha realized he didn't feel quite as bad as he should. The Troll Queen was finally getting a dose of her own medicine. And it felt really, really good.

He met her angered glare head on. No longer would she use fear to make him do what she wanted. Donnacha had been bound in chains for so many years, he'd almost forgotten what it felt like to be free. She wasn't going to like this new version of him.

The Queen reached out and took her daughter's hand. "Now, dear, don't fret. You don't have to marry a man to control him completely and utterly."

"I don't?"

"Of course not. He's already our little slave to toy with as we wish. What he wants doesn't matter. What you want matters." The queen stroked her daughter's face, running a long-nailed finger from forehead to jaw. "My beautiful little girl."

Gods, he didn't even like being in the same room with them. They made him sick. Or maybe that was the smell of the rotting food in the corner. Either way, he didn't want to linger here longer than he had to. Which meant he had to finish what he'd started.

"Sure," he said, raising a brow, "listen to your mother. But I think any young, remarkable woman such as yourself should have a wedding."

"What's that?" the princess asked, turning skeptical eyes to her mother.

Ah, so the princess didn't exactly trust the queen. Not surprising since most trolls ate their young, at least a few. The queen only had the one child. No one else had fathered a sibling with her, and he couldn't blame the princess for not trusting her mother. He could play off the tension between them.

Donnacha lifted a hand. "Only the most extravagant ball a faerie could throw. In the courts, weddings are planned for years. The bride will wear a gown of white gossamer, so beautiful it makes the crowd cry. The groom is dressed in a suit that fits the bride's request, and then he places a ring on her finger more lovingly than the stars in the sky."

Poetry seemed to work on the creature in front of him. The princess's eyes glazed over as she imagined the tale he painted. He had a feeling she was more interested in the crowd adoring her than the rest of it, but he knew how to captivate an audience when he wanted to.

"And the dwarves..." He stepped forward, forcing her gaze back to him. "We sing a wedding song that is more beautiful than any other, a song from the soul, pledging ourselves to the woman we love."

She leaned forward, nearly falling out of her chair before snapping out of it. The princess nearly threw herself at her mother. "Mommy! I want a wedding! Exactly the wedding he said. I want to be the most beautiful woman in all the land."

The Troll Queen held her daughter in her arms and stared at him with malice in her gaze. She hated him. Of that, Donnacha was certain.

But she could deny her daughter nothing.

The Troll Queen held the princess against her skeletal chest and nodded at Donnacha. "Fine. If it's a wedding you want, then it's a wedding you will get. Until then, Donnacha of the dwarven clans, you shall stay in my daughter's room with her, pleasing her every whim."

He shook his head. "I'm afraid I can't, your majesty. Rules of a wedding forbid the groom see the bride the days before."

The princess immediately pulled back and snarled at him. "I'll see you beforehand, or there will be no wedding."

"Then you must remain pure." He hated the words rolling off his tongue. What was a pure woman? Was it possible for anyone to remain so, simply because no man had touched them? "Otherwise, the marriage is nothing more than an elaborate play."

"I like plays," the princess said with a huff.

"But the faerie courts do not."

He had her there. He could see the moment when she agreed with him and decided she'd listen to all he had to say. It didn't matter that he was lying through his teeth. He couldn't lie with this woman who wanted little more than to rape him.

The first time he'd seen her, she had ordered a hundred doves so she could tear their heads off their bodies while alive. The second time he'd seen her, delivering jewelry his father had made, she had called on another troll to scrub her feet, then kicked the troll black and blue when it didn't scrub hard enough.

He refused to entertain the whims of not only a childish person, but a cruel one at that.

The Troll Queen sneered at him then nodded to one of her guards. "You'll stay in the dungeon then. Where bars can keep you two apart, but she'll be able to see your pretty face whenever she wishes."

"Oh, Mommy, thank you!"

14

"Why did the king want her anyway?"

"Well, I don't know the answer to that any more than you do! Just keep your trap shut, and then our debt is paid."

"I don't think it's right to be dragging a lady through the kingdom when she's not even awake. What if he wants her for some nefarious deeds?"

Elva snapped awake as quickly as she'd been knocked out. She regulated her breathing, deepening it so the creatures around her wouldn't realize she could hear them now. They didn't need to fight just yet. She wanted to know what they were up to.

One of them jostled her head. "The king of the dwarves? He's not likely to want her for anything other than questioning. The man is loyal to his people to a fault. She probably did something to hurt 'em."

"Hurt them? Her? Look at her. She's nothing more than a little slip of a girl."

He was wrong about that. Elva knew she was a lot larger than she'd been in the bad old days when her frame had been much more feminine and not quite so muscular. He could have a pass for the comment, as long as they let her go the moment she opened her eyes.

The one to her left, the one with the higher pitched voice who wanted to sell her off like a prized horse, snorted. "Oh if the king of the dwarves wants her, she's a lot more than some little slip of a girl. I wouldn't be surprised if she was some kind of faerie royalty."

"What, is he collecting those kinds of faeries now?"

"Just know he's got a chip on his shoulder about the whole thing. Last time he saw one, they stole the legendary sword of Nuada."

Ah, that would be Eamonn, the current king of the Seelie Court. He'd taken the sword back when he was fighting Elva's ex-husband, his twin brother. The sword could control an entire battlefield with just a thought. It was rumored to control the minds of anyone around it. From what she'd heard of his battles, the sword could actually do that.

The other man to her right with a deep voice picked up her limp arm and waved it at the other creature. "How dare you? He's a good man, and he wants to help people. That's what he's always told us."

"And you believed him?"

"Of course, I believed him. He's got no reason to lie."

Gods, they were like an old married couple. Elva tried to sense where she was, but could only figure out that they'd placed her body on a cart. It shook down a dirt path while the wheels squeaked.

She cracked her eyes open just a bit. The man to the left was dressed in a red hat and a matching cape that fluttered around him. He walked next to the cart with a scowl on his remarkably grotesque face. He was round as a berry with light fur dusting his entire body. A tail wriggled behind him, prehensile and clearly agitated.

Damn. Far darrig.

They were the worst sort of faeries to deal with and known to be the most sluttish, slouching, jeering, mischievous phantoms. They were going to sell her off to the highest bidder, and she didn't have a chance to argue for herself.

Not because she was going to stay silent. Elva had no intention of that. But because far darrig were far beyond reasoning with. They didn't care about her or anyone else.

Opening her eyes completely, she jerked her hands from her lap. Tied. Damn it they'd thought of everything.

Of all the faeries the dwarven king could have sent after her, he had to send the smart ones. Wandering faeries knew how to capture others. They had no allegiance to any court and thus were completely untouchable by any threats of a court reprimand.

Angrily, she snarled at the one with the deeper voice. "I'm going to tear out every hair on your body," she threatened. "One by one until you regret ever taking me."

He held up his hand, the long snout at the end of his face twitching with laughter. "Oh, I'm terrified. Just get out of those ropes first, love, would you?"

She wasn't happy, and she intended to make good on those threats the moment they untied her. And they would have to untie her to fulfil their promise. The dwarven king wouldn't want her lying down on a cart.

Elva tugged at the ropes again. "Where are we?"

"The Otherworld."

Well, at least she was home. Elva stared up at the trees with leaves shaped like stars and realized how much she hated this land. The Otherworld had become a place where she'd been turned into something other than herself. Something pretty and proper who was expected to simper and follow orders.

No more. She wasn't that woman, and she didn't have to be if she didn't want to be. Unless, of course, her mother got her claws back into her.

She couldn't stay here long.

Lying flat, she blew out a breath. "Release me, and I'll double whatever he's paying you."

The one on the left chuckled. "Little girl, I don't think you could really afford us."

"My mother is known as the Duchess of Light in the courts. Perhaps you've heard of her and my father? Illumin is his name. He can do almost anything you want him to."

The far darrig leaned over her until his whiskers touched her cheek. "Can he get our brother away from the dwarven king? Oh, and maybe convince Angus that it's a bad idea to go to war with the wandering faeries? Maybe also give us a royal pardon for sneaking into the cellars of the Seelie King and stealing almost every sword he had just to see whether or not he still had the sword of Nuada?"

She stared into his beady eyes and felt her mouth twist in disgust. "No."

"Then I think we're at an impasse, princess." He patted her cheek. "But it's good to know you're worth money for when the dwarven king is done with you. Maybe we'll take you back and ransom you to dear ol' Mummy and Daddy."

Gods, she hated wandering fae. They were usually weak creatures who were cast out of their courts, unless they were these creatures. Related yet again to the leprechaun, far darrig were creatures without laws.

Why was she meeting so many creatures related to leprechauns lately?

"Shut up," she snarled.

"Gladly. I didn't want to talk to you anyway. You're boring."

The rest of the trip was passed in silence other than the sounds of Elva twisting the ropes around her wrists. She wanted to get out, to be able to save herself. However, these creatures really did know what they were doing. They'd tied her so successfully, she wasn't sure she could have gotten out of these ties with days at her disposal.

Thankfully, the journey wasn't days long. Just as the sun was setting on the horizon, the far darrig stopped the cart, clicked their heels together, and slapped their foreheads with their hands.

When they remained completely still, she sighed. "What are you doing?"

"Hush, the king approaches."

"Care to tell me why you're holding your foreheads then?"

The hissed response made even less sense. "It shows respect! You should do the same, faerie princess."

Elva didn't have it in her to try and explain that, first of all, they shouldn't be holding their foreheads. Their hands should be at an angle to their skull, a salute. And second of all, her hands were still tied.

A voice interrupted them, the age-old sound of a mountain groaning. She hadn't ever heard a voice so deep or so filled with pleasure. "Thank you, far darrig. You've done a wonderful job. I shall offer you my services as repayment."

"A job well done indeed, your majesty. You asked for the woman, and we supplied her."

"Supplied" was a harsh word. They'd taken her from the rubble of the castle when she'd fallen beneath it. But sure, they could take credit for destroying an entire magical building created by the creature who had cursed Donnacha.

Elva ground her teeth and stared up at the first stars poking through the sky. Rolling her lips between her teeth, she tried to wipe away her expression that clearly conveyed she was fed up. Done. She didn't want to be around faeries ever again.

Crunching footsteps approached her.

She wasn't going to look. It didn't matter if the far darrig wanted to say goodbye to her or if it was the dwarven king himself. They could all go suck an elf for all she cared.

A face blocked out the stars from her sight. Angus, the king of the dwarves, was very much as she remembered. She'd only met him once at a ball when his people were still part of the Seelie court, but he was just as handsome. His beard had speckles of gray, but his vivid blue eyes were still as pretty as before. Now, she saw something familiar in the wrinkles at the corners of his eyes and the dimples on his cheeks.

"Hello, Elva," he said. "Fancy seeing you here."

"I thought I'd go for a stroll. Lovely night for a walk."

"Little hard to walk with your hands tied."

She looked down at her wrists. "Oh this? New fashion statement. It's all the rage in the courts, but you wouldn't know that, would you?"

"Ah, I thank the stars every day I don't." He nodded at her wrists as well. "Shall I?"

"I'd be ever so grateful," she said sarcastically.

Angus reached into his pocket and pulled out a knife. The dim light of the moon reflected off the sharp edge. She'd seen dwarven-made blades like this before. They could cut through anything. Literally, anything.

Once, she'd seen another faerie use it on three-foot thick stone. The blade had cut through it like butter and left a seared edge glowing red.

She must have made some noise because Angus looked up with an amused expression. "Easy, faerie. I've no intention of cutting through you as well."

"Doesn't mean you won't slip."

"Do I look like the kind of man who slips?"

If he was anything like his cousin, no. And she was certain Donnacha and Angus were related now. If she'd had any doubt, the mischief in his smile would have told her everything she needed to know.

The far darrig bolted the moment he started to saw through her bindings. Elva glared after them, praying she would someday have the time to hunt them down.

"Oh, go easy on them," Angus said with a laugh. "They were just doing what they were told."

"Doesn't mean they had to hogtie me."

"Would you have come otherwise?"

The moment she was free, she sat up, looking around, rubbing her wrists. This was the entrance to the dwarven kingdom. She'd heard of the great carved warriors standing outside the opening to the giant mine. She'd just never thought it would be so big.

Everything here was beautifully made but roughly hewn. Clearly designed with masculine intent, every bit of this place was terrifying. The dim light, the scowls on the warriors faces as they held swords aloft. Even the dark abyss awaiting her in that hole.

Elva shook her head. "No, probably not."

"Then I'm afraid you really left me no choice." Angus held out his hand for her to take. "Here, let me help you."

As if she was going to touch him that easily. Elva ignored the offered appendage and hopped down from the wooden cart herself. "Thanks."

He looked down at his hand and then at her. "You're welcome?"

Elva wiped her hands on her pants. Gods, she didn't even like the idea of touching him. It instantly made her palms slick with sweat. "What do you want, Angus?"

"Why don't we go somewhere more comfortable to talk?" He gestured toward the hole in the mountain and reached forward to place his hand on her shoulder blade.

She knew he didn't mean it to be an aggressive gesture. She knew most people would have taken the assistance with a grain of salt. He was trying to be supportive, to give her a chance to lean on someone after her mistreatment.

But her mind didn't think like that. Instead, her hand snapped out to meet his, and she yanked his fingers back so hard she felt them pop. "Do not touch me."

He let out a sound somewhere between gasp and chuckle. "All right then, that's fine. I just thought you'd like to sit down after that unfortunate journey."

"The one you ordered to happen."

"I'll admit I didn't expect them to treat you like that—"

"That's exactly what you expected. Don't even try to twist your words with me Angus. What do you want?"

He reached out with his free hand and gently pried her off him. Shaking the wounded fingers, he shook his head. "My, but you are a terrifying thing now, aren't you?"

"I'm not in the mood for games."

"Neither am I. You were with my cousin, were you not? Donnacha?"

Elva nodded.

"Then I think we both have the same plan. I don't know what you did to anger the Troll Queen like you did, but she's most definitely got him now, and that I cannot stand for."

"Wait," Elva held up her hand. "The Troll Queen cursed him?"

"He didn't tell you?"

"He couldn't." Everything made so much more sense now. Of course, it had to be someone like the Troll Queen. That curse hadn't been entirely intelligent, but it was most certainly effective. The woman had somehow managed to bind Donnacha to herself and then wrapped the curse in whatever safety nets she could.

Efficient, but certainly not the best way to trap someone else.

Elva looked at Angus, then back at the hole in the ground. She really didn't want to go into the mines. They were dark, and faeries liked to see the sky more than anything else. Sighing, she shook her head and stalked toward the abyss. "Fine, talk while you walk."

She swore he grumbled, "I don't understand what he sees in you."

Ignoring whatever words he had said, she pointed toward their destination. "What do I have to do?"

"Walk?"

"Is there some kind of pulley system to lower us into the ground?"

"No."

Elva nearly stumbled over a root. "Excuse me? Everyone says the dwarves live underground."

He shrugged and overtook her. Though his legs were shorter, he was a surprisingly quick little dwarf. "You shouldn't believe everything you hear. That's the entrance to the dwarven kingdom, but I don't want everyone else to see you. They aren't particularly fond of Donnacha, and helping him would anger a few people I don't want to anger."

"Really?" Elva followed Angus into the bushes and to the side of a stone warrior. "Who's that?"

Between the feet of the giant sculpture, a small hut stood. A fire burned merrily behind the windows and smoke rose from the brick chimney. Thick logs made up the walls, and a small rocking chair sat outside the dark wood door.

Quaint, really. She might have even liked the home if she wasn't so upset.

Angus strode to the front door and held it open for her. "There are a lot of dwarves who think someone cursed is beyond our help. We should leave them to their own devices because, if we let them come home, they'll bring the curse back with them."

"Not if you break it," she grumbled as she strode past him.

"Try explaining that to the ancient dwarves, would you? I haven't had much luck."

"No, thank you for the opportunity, though." She'd rather burn off her fingertips. Dwarves were annoying at best, and downright rude at worst.

The interior of the hut was as cute as the outside. Checkered blankets covered a small cot in the corner. Burning logs filled a stone fireplace on the back wall, and twin chairs sat next to the dancing flames.

Angus gestured to one of the chairs. "Food? Water?"

"Both." She sank onto the fur-covered rocker and stared into the fire. What was she doing here? There was always the option of going home. She could walk right back to the Seelie court and into her old life. But she didn't want that. She didn't even know where *home* was anymore.

Although, Donnacha had been teaching her what that meant.

Angus returned, handed her a goblet full of water and a loaf of bread, then sat down beside her. "What do you want with Donnacha?"

She raised a brow. "Try again with another question."

"No, I want to know. You were at that castle for an awfully long time, and you'll have to excuse me when I say I don't trust you. I don't think you were there because you saw some poor cursed sap and thought you might help him. So out with it."

"How do you even know all that?"

Angus chuckled. "Dwarves have their ways. He's my cousin, Seelie. I never lost track of him, even in the darkest of times."

Elva busied herself with drinking the water. Then, when he kept staring at her, she shrugged and shook her head. "I don't know what you want me to say."

"You could start with the truth."

"There's no truth. I was there because Scáthach asked me to be."

"And?"

She shoved the bread in her mouth, purposefully chewing with it open when he got too close with the staring. "What's it to you?"

"He's my cousin."

"So? I've seen faeries kill family every day. What does it matter that the Troll Queen has him?" It mattered more than the breath in her lungs. Feeling her expression shift, she looked back at the fire instead of meeting the pain in his gaze.

"You feel something for him," Angus said, leaning back in his chair. "That's what it is."

"I don't know what you're talking about."

"Yes, you do. You feel something for him, and you don't want to let him go."

"I don't feel anything for him. I don't even know the man. He couldn't talk about himself at all, and he was cursed as a bear. Do you really think much talking happened?"

Angus leaned forward. "Then why are you still here, Elva? Why are you here when you could have walked away? Why is there interest in your eyes every time I start talking about saving him?"

He was asking too many questions. He was too close. Had it gotten hot in this small room all of a sudden? She needed to go outside and catch her breath. She needed…

Him.

Donnacha had been the first person who had helped her breathe around another living person. She'd just been getting to the point where she could touch him without feeling like she was going to fly apart.

Why couldn't she feel the same with this dwarf? It didn't make any sense!

She leaned forward and mirrored Angus's position. "Because I'm not done with him yet."

"Sexually?"

"No."

"Emotionally?"

"Hardly."

Angus shook his head. "You've got to give me more than that. Otherwise, I'll save him myself."

"You'll never get close enough to the Troll Queen to touch him."

"Dwarves are much smaller and easier to ignore than a faerie." He laced his fingers together over a knee and tilted his head to the side.

A challenge? Elva leaned back in her chair and rested her hands in her lap. "They already have one dwarf, Angus. Do you think they really won't notice two? They're looking for a dwarf constantly."

"At least I know I can trust one of my own."

"You can't trust anyone," she murmured, feeling the shadows of her past darken her gaze. "As a king, I thought you'd know that."

He let out a long, frustrated sigh. "Fine. Fine, this is probably the stupidest thing I've ever done in my life, but I believe you. You want to find him."

"I do."

"You somehow have made a connection with him that is neither emotional or physical, although I doubt this completely."

She did as well, but he didn't need to know that. As long as Elva kept telling herself there was no connection between them, then there was no connection. She could survive this as she had survived so much more.

Nodding, she stuck out her hand. "Deal. Now, I have to go, so if you can provide me with armor and a sword."

He tilted his head to the side with an unimpressed expression. "Elva. I have been planning this rescue since the first moment Donnacha was cursed. Do you think I don't have a plan?"

"I think if you had a plan, you wouldn't need me."

Angus tilted his head to the other side and nodded. "Well, you aren't wrong there. But I did make a pack for you. Did he tell you where the Troll Kingdom is? It always seems to move."

"East of the sun, west of the moon."

"Right. So an impossible place." Angus scrubbed a hand through his beard, a move Donnacha made right before he was about to suggest something ridiculous. "Well, there are a few people I know who might help."

She knew what he was going to say. She'd had the same thought herself, but she didn't want to owe any other faeries debts, and she most certainly would.

"Do not say—"

"I was going to suggest—"

"Bugganes."

"Bugganes."

Elva threw her hands up in the air. "Absolutely not."

"They are basically trolls," Angus cajoled. "It makes sense they would know where the Troll Kingdom is."

"They aren't trolls. They are stupid, ridiculous creatures who have rocks for brains. I am not going to beg them for a favor. Do you know what they'd do to me?"

Angus gave her a once-over and grinned. "For a lock of your hair, I think they'd do anything."

"How dare you?"

"It's just hair."

She didn't want faeries having a bit of who she was. That was more dangerous than giving them a spell to curse her with. Huffing out a breath, she crossed her arms over her chest. "It's not happening."

He reached under his chair and tossed the pack at her. "Get yourself ready, Elva. The bugganes aren't that far from here."

"I'm not doing it."

"Do you want to find Donnacha?"

Of course, she did. She wanted to understand why he made her feel like a person and not like something broken. She wanted to understand why he made her feel the way she did. Why he made her feel whole when she'd spent so many years certain there were cracks running down her entire being that everyone could see.

Finally, she punched the arm of the chair and stood. "Yes, fine. But you're leading the way, and if they want a deal, you're taking the fall for it."

15

Long nails clicked on the bars to his cell, as they had every morning for the past week. Donnacha knew it had been exactly seven days because he'd scratched a mark on the wall every day he was in this hellish place. Seven marks under the smallest window he'd ever seen.

The cot they'd given him was little more than two boards with fabric stretched between them. It was uncomfortable, though that was likely the point. The Troll Queen wouldn't want him to think this was a good place for him to be. She wanted to punish him for playing his little games.

Still, at least he'd won something over her.

"Huuuusbaaaand!" The word was long and drawn out, sung off tune as the Troll princess made her way toward him.

She'd taken to calling him the name ever since he'd told her about weddings. She'd told him she quite liked the idea of binding him to her for all eternity.

He didn't want to even think about such a fate. He had to cling to the hope that Elva would come for him. Hadn't he asked her to? Hadn't he begged in those last moments when her taste still lingered on his tongue?

Donnacha couldn't imagine she'd just let him go. Of all the women he'd ever known, she was the kind of person to value action. She would want to race after him. To find him.

Right?

The clanging sound echoed so strongly in his cell that he had to turn his head. Looking through the bars at the creature beyond made his stomach roll. Her tusks were even more pronounced today, if that was possible. The straggly hair on her head, really only three clumps, were tied back with a bright pink bow. The frilly dress covering her body flounced with every movement.

He reminded himself that being this shallow served no one well. He didn't need to be attracted to her. Even if she was the most beautiful woman in the world, he couldn't forget her ripping off those poor birds heads. He couldn't forget the mistreatment of her people and the spoiled personality that poisoned her veins. She was a creature whose inner ugliness had poured out into her skin. That was all.

Still, his lip curled up at the sight of her. "What do you want?"

She pouted. "You're supposed to be happy to see me."

"And why would I be happy to see you?"

"Because Mummy said..." She stamped her foot on the ground, obviously frustrated. "You're supposed to do what I say! You're mine."

"A person can't be someone's plaything, princess."

"They can if I make them!" The troll princess smacked her fist against the bars. "If they don't, I'll pound them into the ground until they behave."

"If you pound them into the ground, then they'll be dead." It was like explaining cause and effect to a child. She was older than him! She should know all of this already.

But she didn't. Donnacha reminded himself to be patient. Spoiled rotten and someone whose mother had made her the way she was. He had to be gentler. More understanding.

Even though he didn't want to be.

Donnacha rolled and planted his feet on the ground, rubbing his hands over his face. "What is it you want, princess?"

"We're going to go out today! Isn't it wonderful? Mummy said she wanted everyone in the kingdom to see your failure. It will make us both laugh."

Because the other trolls would attack him? No, they wouldn't risk him to something so foolish as that. Perhaps the Troll Queen had something else up her sleeve, but that didn't matter. He could survive this just as he had the other curse.

He pushed himself to standing and sighed, holding his arms up. "Fine then. When are we going?"

She twirled a finger in the thin threads of her ponytail. "Right now."

"Are you going to dress me in something other than this?" Donnacha had been in the dungeons for an entire week now with nothing more than meager water and bread. He smelled to the high heavens. It was even starting to bother him now, which is when he knew it was getting bad. His beard was a mess, his hair a tangled rat's nest, and his shirt was sticking to his chest from the layers of sweat. He desperately wanted a bath. He needed to feel clean so he could feel like a person again.

The troll princess shook her head. "No, Mum doesn't want you to have a bath. She said let him go as he is." She looked him up and down with hungry eyes. "I agree."

Donnacha scrambled for the right words. "Everyone will think you're marrying a disgusting beast. Is that what you want?"

The troll princess pressed her tiny breasts against the bars. "Are you a beast, dwarf? That's what I like to hear. You'll need to be animalistic to survive when I'm done with you."

Gods, he was going to vomit. He looked for the waste bucket and realized they'd already taken it for the next hour. What was he going to do? Puke straight down her front and ruin all the good he'd done?

He had to continue this plan. The princess had to be in his

back pocket, or everything would fall apart at the seams. She was the one pulling her mother's strings, which meant if he could pull *her* strings, then his life might not be that bad after all.

Donnacha stepped forward. Smiling through the disgust, he said through clenched teeth, "I am looking forward to being seen by your side."

Her eyes glazed over. "Tell me why."

Because he wanted the entire kingdom to remember his face when he escaped. Because he forever wanted to be known as the man who fooled the Troll Queen and her ugly daughter.

Instead of saying all that, Donnacha reached forward and touched a lock of her greasy hair. "That's a secret for me to keep."

"But why?" She pouted. "I want to know what your secret is! I'm good at keeping them."

He was certain that was a lie. She seemed like the kind of creature who would have blabbed whatever she wanted to whomever would listen. But that was all right. He wasn't going to tell her a thing, no matter how much she begged.

Donnacha shook his head and stepped back. "Another time, my bride. Now, let's go out into the world and let the entire kingdom see us."

The troll princess snapped her fingers, and the guards approached. They were much taller than her, blocks of gray stone that hardly looked like they should be able to move. Their armor was made of rock as well, something he'd have to ask his dwarven family how it was possible. He thought perhaps it was magic, which made them all the more dangerous.

He only came up to their hip anyway, it didn't make sense for him to fight. They'd pound him into the ground, as the princess had so eloquently said, before he had any idea what was happening. And he much preferred to stay alive and well.

The troll princess immediately approached him. She smelled like wet earth, mulch that had festered and was now filled with mold. His nose wrinkled, but he stayed where he was. If the guards saw him flinch, they'd likely toss him toward her. And once the princess had her fingers in him, he wasn't sure she'd ever let go.

He winced when she leaned close and sniffed him. "Oh, you're going to be the most lovely pet I've ever had," she murmured.

"Glad to know that."

"You should be much happier to have my attentions, you know. Most people would kill for them."

Or to get away from them, he thought. Semantics really.

She sighed and rolled her eyes. "Come on then, follow me."

He trailed after her and tried his best not to look into the other dungeon cells. He already knew what manner of creatures were there. It might have been easier if he'd seen other faeries of his own kind. If the trolls hated other people more than they hated each other.

That was not the case. Instead, the dungeon was filled with hundreds of other trolls, creatures whose rock-like skin had since cracked from misuse. Whose haunted eyes watched him with curiosity and hunger.

They would have eaten him if he wandered into one of their cells. He was certain of that. One of the creatures had even grown into the wall of his cell. Desperation sometimes led trolls to becoming part of the earth. They thought it was a way for them to get their power back. Unfortunately, it rarely worked. From what Donnacha had heard, it was a fitting death for those who tried to steal from the Otherworld itself.

Up the stairs, they went into a sun that blinded him. He held up a hand to his stinging eyes, shocked at how bright it was. Had it always been daylight here? He'd thought the Troll Kingdom was stormy.

"Donnacha!" the Troll Queen called out. "How lovely to see you're still alive. My daughter hasn't killed you yet, then."

"Your hospitality has left nothing wanting," he muttered.

"Glad to hear it. Tie him onto a horse. Would one of you useless idiots do something for once?"

A guard picked him up under the arms and plopped him on top of the nearest horse. Donnacha scrambled for the reigns, shocked they'd handled him like a child. It was exceedingly rude to just pick up a dwarf. Gods, he hated these people.

Why weren't the others riding? When Donnacha's eyes finally adjusted, he realized the trolls were just…standing there. Waiting for him to be ready. When he was situated, the princess stood next to him. Her head was at his height now, even though he was atop a horse. How large was this woman? He'd forgotten what she looked like while he was in a human form, and not through the fog of a mirror.

Beady eyes stared up at him with far too much interest. "You're much more handsome up close."

"Thank you," he muttered.

The Troll Queen called the march to begin, and the trolls moved forward as one. There weren't gates to the castle. Instead, there was a line of trolls as far as the eye could see standing in front of them in a line.

The princess waved to everyone as she walked, although she didn't look as though she truly recognized any of them. In fact, no one seemed happy to be there at all. The trolls on the sidelines were glaring at the others as if they wanted to start a fight.

Donnacha tried to remember his limited knowledge of these creatures. There weren't nobles other than the royal family. Which meant the creatures walking with him had to be chosen by the queen. Such a choice would certainly make some of them very uncomfortable. In fact, he could tell they wanted to see blood spilled.

He didn't need to get caught in the middle of a troll fight. He wouldn't survive.

Blowing out a nervous breath, he glanced around, watching

for any kind of weapon to be drawn. So far, he was lucky that no one threw a fist. But there was a long way to go.

He desperately wished for his own weapons. A sword, an axe, anything that he could have thrown at an enemy or sank between a troll's ribs. Swords weren't likely to cut through troll flesh, but a man could dream.

Then he saw it. The sudden flash of light that was too bright to be a troll and far too vivid to be something troll-made.

Gold.

She was here. That had to be her. He tried not to crane his neck to stare through the crowd of trolls, but he was certain that was Elva. It had to be.

He twisted in the saddle only to have his face caught in the hand of the troll princess. "What are you looking at?"

"Nothing."

"There isn't another troll here who's more beautiful than me. You've already got the best one." Her fingers squeezed his jaw painfully. "Stare at me if you wish to stare."

Donnacha winced, then looked forward. "You've got it, bride of mine."

Stomach churning, he watched the road in front of them for the rest of the ride. Was she here? Had she finally made it?

16

Elva crouched in the bushes beside Angus. The bugganes were so close she could smell them, and it wasn't a pleasant smell in the slightest. She forced her hand to stay at her side instead of covering her mouth as she desperately wanted to.

"Well, we're here," she hissed. "Now what?"

Angus silenced her with a glare and then pointedly stared at the bugganes mere steps from them.

They were gigantic creatures who were sorely lacking in looks. Covered entirely with coarse black fur, they looked more like animals than fae. Of course, their glowing red eyes and large tusks curving up from their bottom lip didn't help either.

Three of them stood in front of the bushes, muttering about some food they needed to find. Or cook? Elva had a hard time understanding them when the tusks made their words lisp.

Elva leaned closer to Angus so the bugganes wouldn't hear her speak. "What's the plan?"

"We wait until we have an opening."

"I think there's an opening in front of us."

"They will kill us if we barge into their camp. They aren't

exactly the most intelligent of creatures and are prone to knee-jerk reactions."

She arched a brow. "Are you afraid of them?"

He jerked as if she had shot him. "Afraid of bugganes?"

"It seems like you are."

"I'm not afraid of faeries."

Right. She somehow very much didn't believe that when he was already casting a nervous glance at the three bugganes who might overhear them.

"I should never have doubted you, Your Majesty. My apologies." Elva shook her head at him, then stood up.

"What are you doing?" he hissed, tugging at her pant leg.

"Finishing this." She didn't have time to waste because he was afraid of what these creatures might do. Who cared if the beasts wanted to fight them? She had a sword and had the training to take them down. Somehow, she doubted they would attack them on sight.

Bugganes might be terrifying-looking creatures, but they weren't as stupid as trolls. They knew how to speak with others and had created an entire homeland for themselves. They didn't attack faeries; they didn't cause trouble. In fact, most of the other faerie species had forgotten they existed at all.

That didn't seem to be a race of creatures who wanted to hurt others. Not in her experience with the rather dangerous and terrifying Seelie Court.

She strode from the bushes, shaking off Angus's hand, and made her way toward the three bugganes.

"Good morning," she called out. "I'd like to ask you a question if I might."

The buggane closest to her immediately fluffed up. Its fur pointed out in all directions and it whirled on her with a growl that blasted Elva's hair back from her face.

Closing her eyes for a moment, she wiped away a spot of spit that had stuck to her cheek. "Well, that's one way to welcome visitors."

The other two bugganes loomed closer, while the one who had growled straightened. "Who are you trespassing upon our lands?"

"My name is Elva. Lovely to meet you." She held out the hand which was now slick, resolving to wipe the creatures own bodily fluids back on it.

The buggane reached forward and shook her hand.

They were suspicious of her, and she couldn't really blame for them. After all, it was a dangerous thing to see another faerie wander into their territory without reason. And she was wearing a sword to boot. She just hoped they didn't think she was going to attack them. She didn't want to have to draw said sword any time soon.

"I need you to take me to the troll kingdom," she said. It was better to simply say why she was there than keep them waiting.

The buggane holding her hand coughed. "You what?"

"The Troll Queen has someone who is very important to me in her dungeons, I assume, and I want him back. I've been told you are the only creatures who know how to get there."

"We're not taking you to the troll kingdom."

Elva blinked. "Why not?"

"Well, it's dangerous ma'am."

"The kingdom or the journey?"

The buggane looked over its shoulder at the other creatures behind it, clearly confused at the direction this conversation was going. "Both?"

"You don't sound very confident in that answer. I need you to be more confident."

"I—well—you see—"

Elva interrupted the creature, not quite pleased with how it was responding. "I need to go now. There's no time to waste. Can one of you take me, or do I need to ask someone else?"

The largest buggane of the group stepped forward, peering

over the other's shoulder with beady, glowing eyes. "Who *are* you?"

"I've already told you that."

"Yes, but...aren't you afraid of us?"

"No." She shrugged. "I don't think I'm afraid of much, honestly."

Her hand dropped as the closest buggane backed into its friend away from her. "What manner of creature are you?"

"Seelie."

"And you aren't afraid of the troll kingdom?"

Elva pretended to think about the question, then shook her head. "No."

"Why not?"

"I need my friend back, and fear is only going to stand in my way. He taught me that letting fear rule my life is a waste of time. And I want him back."

"Why do you want him back?" The buggane leaned closer until Elva could smell the wet dog scent of its fur. "What is he to you?"

Gods, she didn't know how to answer that. There were too many avenues she could take. Instead, she ended up being truthful. "I don't really know, to be honest. But I'd like to find out, so I need you to take me to him. I need to find out what he is to me."

The buggane clasped its hands to its chest and sighed. "Oh, a love story."

Elva held up her hand. "That's not what I said—"

"You love him!"

"I really don't think that's the reason I want to find him, and besides—"

The buggane held up its hand, mirroring her movements and censoring her with a harsh look. "We love love stories. There's nothing we honor more than a woman trying to find her mate."

Her mate? She didn't have a mate, and Elva didn't believe in soulmates to begin with. Love was finding someone she could stand living with until she couldn't stand them anymore.

But then again…maybe it wasn't. Maybe she was wrong.

"Oh!" The buggane turned and slapped the shoulder of the one behind her. "Did you see? Did you see the moment she realized?"

"I don't love him," Elva said again. It wasn't possible that she loved him. They'd only known each other under strange circumstances and for such a short time. She'd have to be mad to fall in love with a man that quickly.

Even if he was kind and thoughtful. Even if he understood what was going through her mind, and when he didn't, he gave her the space to figure it out on her own. It didn't matter that he'd seen more than just her beauty but her strength as well, and no one else had ever seen that in her. That didn't matter. It couldn't be love. Not this soon.

The buggane watched her carefully and then nodded firmly. "I'll take you."

One of the other creatures, the one who hadn't spoken yet, whispered, "My love—"

"No." The buggane shook her head. Elva was certain it was a "she" now. "I've made up my mind. I want to take her. And in return, she'll tell me the entire story so I can tell the others over the fire."

A small price to pay. Elva glanced back at the bushes she'd come out of and signaled a thumbs up to Angus. The dwarf wasn't visible, but she was certain he was watching. She hadn't wanted him to come with her anyway. This was a journey that was far better off on her own.

"All right," Elva said. "Do you need to get ready?"

"Not at all." The buggane held out its arms. "Come along, faerie. I'll carry you the whole way."

She was going to have to be close to all that wet fur? Elva tried not to wrinkle her nose. It would take her years to wash the smell off her skin. The things she was doing for this foolish dwarf who'd gotten himself into a ridiculous mess. Donnacha had better appreciate her efforts to find him.

Elva stepped into the creature's arms and let it sweep her up. The journey was swift, over the hills and dales as only a buggane could run. Elva was shocked at the creature's pace. She'd known bugganes were quick, but she hadn't realized their magic was in their ability to travel from place to place.

The creature ran like the wind itself was underneath its feet. They raced past villages without a single person seeing them. The fur rustled around her, but it didn't seem as though they were running that fast. She would have thought it was only a comfortable lope if she hadn't seen the earth moving by them so quickly.

"Tell me the story," the buggane whispered, its voice somehow easy to hear even though they were running.

And so, Elva did.

She left out no detail, even her own emotions that she hadn't given words to yet. She poured all her abilities of storytelling into the tale. She embellished the cursed bear, the ice castle, the places outside of the world they knew.

Each moment she said something remotely romantic, the buggane would sigh in her ear. Elva admitted the story did seem fantastical. Now, she was racing to the man's side so that they could defeat the Troll Queen and take down a kingdom of evil creatures who punished those who didn't deserve to be punished.

She'd never been a woman who wanted to be a hero. In the beginning, she just wanted to live a quiet life of luxury, and then it turned into wanting a life that was just quiet, solitary. Elva had wanted to learn how to protect herself, to push everyone away so no one could hurt her again.

Until a bear appeared. A terrifying, monstrous creature who could have torn her limb from limb easily. Except, he hadn't. He'd been kind, sweet, and generous in his ability to understand her pain and hardship.

By the time they stopped, she felt as though all her emotions had been wrung out. Maybe they had. She didn't know how the bugganes found their magic. Perhaps, they were creatures who ate stories like this.

The buggane let her down and patted the top of her head. "You've done well, little faerie. Now, go find your man."

"But where are we?"

The buggane pointed down the hill they were on. "There's your troll kingdom. Might I suggest starting with the princess? She's your best bet at learning how to get in there."

As the creature behind her raced away, Elva feasted her eyes on the kingdom below. Stone buildings, roughly hewn and clearly without any guidance, dotted the horizon. Twin lines of creatures stood at the roadside, and they were more disgusting than she'd ever seen before. She thought the bugganes were hard to look at? The trolls were even worse.

Stone hides, leather, bark, all the textures that shouldn't have been on a creature's body. Not to mention the sparse hair growing in places it shouldn't grow, the small eyes, the tusks, even strange second limbs poking out of backs.

These creatures were more than just disgusting. They were grotesque.

Elva reached into the pack Angus had given her and dragged out a cloak. It would cover her form enough for her to see what was going on. All the trolls were lined up like they were waiting for something, and she needed to know what that was.

Throwing the fabric over her shoulders, she slid down the hill and into the crowds of trolls.

No one looked at her. In fact, they weren't even looking at each other. They were staring at a procession coming down the hill.

Trolls? She hadn't thought they would have a procession like that. They weren't exactly known to like each other, and having an entire kingdom watching them would only invite battles no one wanted to deal with. So what in the world were they doing?

The guards at the front certainly looked worried. Their eyes scanned the crowds for any movement that would threaten their royals. And that was definitely the Troll Queen who strode at the head of the procession with an arrogant grin on her face and without a care in the world.

The buggane had said to look for the troll princess. Who would be the princess? She looked for someone that appeared similar to the queen, but no one was as skeletal as that creature.

"Donnacha," she whispered as she saw the horse.

He sat on the creature, who clearly wanted to bolt at his earliest chance. The troll next to him was little more than a boulder with hair, but Elva was certain that was the princess. She was too confident in her movements to be anyone else.

Donnacha looked worse for the wear. His hair was matted on his head, and the miserable look on his face was clearly exhaustion and something else. Something she didn't want to put a name to because it looked very much like he'd given up.

She squeezed between two very large trolls and nudged the hood of her cloak back just enough to flash her hair. No one else could see her, but she had to let him know she was here. The light returned to his eyes. He twisted in the saddle, searching for her with hope back in his gaze..

That wouldn't do. Not yet. Elva had to figure out her plan, and that started with the troll princess. She faded back into the crowd and slowly followed the procession until it turned back around and returned to the towering castle made of stone.

She could start here. Elva had learned how to be patient. Thankfully, her mentor had instilled that in her. She waited for her moment, following the trolls silently as a wraith. She peered through windows, stepping lightly around the castle to assess every angle of her first attack.

The trolls went back into the castle. They shoved Donnacha down some stairs that must have led to the dungeon, and then they all went to feast.

She couldn't go into the feast herself. They'd find her, and then everything would be over before it started. So Elva set herself at a window and pulled out an apple from her pack. It felt heavier than before, but she wasn't in any position to go through what Angus had sent.

Then, her opportunity arose. The troll princess stood from the drunken revelries and weaved her way through the crowd and out through a back door.

Elva held the apple in her mouth, put the pack back on, and threw the cloak over her shoulders. Rushing around the castle, she stuck to the shadows until she found the troll princess using the bushes as a bathroom.

Rolling her eyes, she leaned against the wall of the castle and made sure the hood covered her face. When the princess finished, Elva took a large, loud bite out of the apple.

The troll princess froze, but didn't drop into a protective stance as many other trolls would have done. Interesting. Did the creature not know how to fight?

"Who goes there?" the princess asked, her voice wavering in fear.

"No one."

The princess stamped her foot on the ground. "You aren't no one! I can hear you."

Elva watched the confusion on the princess's face and realized two things. First, this creature had little to no intelligence in her head. That was good. It meant she was easily manipulated. And second, the troll princess was little more than a spoiled child who grew angry when someone made her feel foolish.

Elva took a step out of the shadows and took another bite of her apple. "Strange, cause I just said I'm no one."

"W—what do you want?"

"I want to know about the dwarf you have captured. Where is he?"

The troll princess crossed her arms over her chest. "I'm not talking about my toy. You want it for yourself? Go find yourself another one."

A toy? What had Donnacha gotten himself into?

Elva shrugged. "Suit yourself then. I'll find out from someone else who wants a gift from me."

"A gift?" The troll princess stepped forward. "I like gifts."

"So do I. But my gift is only for the person who tells me why that dwarf is here."

"What's it to you?"

Elva shrugged again, biting into the apple a little more aggressively than before. "I'm curious, that's all."

"What's the gift then?"

Really, she only had another apple to give the troll princess. The creature might be a little more intelligent than she gave her credit for if she was asking to know what the gift was. Elva stretched her arm back and reached underneath the cloak for the apple. She'd have to make up a story about how it was a magical apple or something...

Wait a minute. Her fingers grazed an apple, but it was too smooth and cold. She palmed it, realizing the apple was heavier than the other as well. She furrowed her brows, grateful the troll princess couldn't see her expressions, and pulled out the strange object.

A golden apple, so pure and smooth it looked as though it had been plucked from the branches of a magical tree.

It almost made Elva breathless in its beauty. Angus was a crafty dwarf after all, she mused.

Holding up the exquisite piece, she let the light of the moon reflect on it. "A gift for the person who tells me why the dwarf is here and lets me have a few moments alone with him."

The troll princess watched the golden apple with greedy eyes. "I want it."

"You can have it, if you give me what I want."

"Mummy says no one else can know the dwarf is here." The

troll princess chewed on her lip and held out her hand. "But no one else has that."

"That's because this apple is one of a kind. No one else in the Otherworld or the human realms has ever seen anything like it. It's made of magic and so much power you can feel it when you're holding it." Elva turned it in her fingers. "Isn't it beautiful?"

"It is."

"Then do you want it?"

The troll princess jumped once, making the ground shake. "I do!"

"Why is the dwarf here?"

"To marry me. Mummy said I could have any mate I wanted for my children, and I picked him. The dwarf said marriage was better than just a mate, so we're going to have a wedding. I don't like waiting, but he said it was better. Can I have it now?"

Crafty. Donnacha had made himself enough time for her to get here. That was far more useful than experiencing whatever the mating process would be with this creature.

Elva shook her head. "Not yet. I want to see the dwarf for myself. Can you do that?"

"Mummy said no!"

"Do you always do what your mother tells you to do? You're the princess, aren't you?"

The troll princess took a few steps forward, hands reaching out and fingers curling in the air. "I want it."

"Then give me a few minutes with the dwarf. I'm not going to do anything. I just want to see this husband of yours for myself."

"Fine," the troll princess snarled. "I'll take you to him."

Elva tossed the golden apple to the troll and took another bite out of her own. "Lead the way."

17

He should never have drank anything the Troll princess gave him, but Donnacha hadn't really had that much of a choice, now had he? She'd practically run into the dungeons with her beady eyes wider than he thought they could go. She'd thrust water at him, insisting he drink it, and then poured it down his throat when he hadn't wanted to.

Donnacha only had a moment to taste the strange bitters before he felt his eyes roll back in his head. Damned trolls. They were always meddling, but he hadn't thought they were capable of poison.

The troll princess had caught him on the way down, stroked his hair, and then whispered in his ear, "I wish we had more time like this. I like you better when your mouth isn't open."

Now, he was laid out haphazardly on his cot, wondering what the hell had just happened. He couldn't even move his head or open his eyes, then the princess leaves? What was she planning?

The cell door opened, and he wanted to tense up. He hated being this weak. Anyone could walk in here and do whatever they wanted, and there was nothing he could do to prevent it. He was stuck, frozen in this moment and panicking. Who was it?

Light footsteps approached him. Light? That wasn't the right sound for a troll. And there weren't any other people here *but* trolls. They didn't let anyone else in their castle. Which could only mean…

"Donnacha," a familiar, soft voice whispered.

She'd found him. His warrior woman had really done it! She'd infiltrated the troll kingdom, made her way all the way east of the sun, west of the moon and somehow tricked the troll princess in allowing them a few moments together.

Was there anything this woman couldn't do?

He desperately strained to move his head, to open his eyes so he could really see her, the most beautiful woman in the world as far as he was concerned. And not because of her looks, although he'd like to see something more than just trolls for the first time in weeks. But because of her beautiful strength, her attitude toward life, and her resolve to never let anything stop her. She was a remarkable woman, and he wanted to tell her that.

"Donnacha?" she asked again, her voice growing worried. "Please tell me you're not dead."

Don't cry, he wanted to say. Please don't cry when he wasn't dead at all. She had to realize he was just asleep, that the troll princess was trying to trick her. They might be dumb creatures, but they could lie unlike the other faerie species who couldn't.

He felt a hand on his throat, fingers pressed against his rapid heartbeat. Panic had the organ inside his chest trying to beat its way out to her.

"Ah," Elva whispered. "All right then. Not dead, just drugged. I didn't think the troll princess would stoop so low."

He knew the troll would. The woman was capable of much more than anyone gave her credit for. A princess was still a dangerous woman when she wanted to be.

Elva leaned down and pressed her lips close to his ear. He felt the sweep of fabric against his cheekbone. Was she wearing a cloak? Something to conceal her form?

"I'm going to get you out. I don't know how yet, but it's going to happen. I need you to be ready for that moment."

Oh, he was readier than she would ever know. He wanted out of this damned place.

She touched her hand to the side of his face and breathed out a sigh. "I wish I could know if you were hearing me at all. If you can hear me, Donnacha, I'm not giving up just yet. Even a dungeon can't keep me away from you. I'm going to get you out of here."

Couldn't keep her away from him? What did that mean? It wasn't possible she felt the strange connection between them as he did. There was so much between them that he couldn't breathe sometimes, but was it possible that both of them felt…?

He swept the thought from his mind. He refused to even consider the strange emotions. It wasn't worth the wasted effort when he couldn't even look at her right now.

Heavy footsteps approached the dungeon, and he heard Elva suck in a deep breath. "I have to go. I'll be back. Be ready."

Oh, he would be ready. He could face a den of lions now that he knew for certain she was here. She was going to get him out, and he would return to the waking world with a renewed sense of vigor.

He could survive this as long as she was beside him.

Donnacha listened to her leave the cell, gently close the gates behind her, and then the fading sound of her sneaking away. No one else would have heard those footsteps. Elva was impossible to hear when she didn't want to be heard.

Except by him. He knew the sound of her sneaking. He'd heard it in the castle for so many months now. He knew how to find her when she didn't want to be found.

Then other footsteps rang through the dungeon. Footsteps he also recognized and hated more than any other.

The Troll Queen approached.

Donnacha's chest seized. This was the worst person to be

alone with. She'd want to kill him, or maim him, or give him to her daughter while he couldn't do anything.

He'd never thought to know what Elva had endured firsthand. The helplessness of immobility. The fear of what another person would do to him while he was still awake. The drug wasn't even beginning to wear off. He still couldn't move, couldn't do anything other than wheeze in a breath that was a hair deeper than the other.

The Troll Queen leaned down at his side, her claws dragging down the length of his arm. "Oh, my dear dwarf, this is how I like to see you."

When he didn't respond, she laughed. He hated her all the more in that moment, a burning contempt that made his chest ache and his head hurt. He wanted to destroy her. He wanted to run a blade between her ribs and feel her blood pour out over his hands. How dare she? How dare she laugh in this moment when he was incapacitated?

The Troll Queen touched his face with her claw. "I want you to know that I saw her. It's not hard to see when someone new is in this kingdom. I know every troll and every rock they are made out of."

She knew Elva was here? Did that mean she was going to attack her?

He wanted to shout for Elva to run. It didn't matter that he needed saving. The Troll Queen would never let him go, and he couldn't bear be the reason she could be caught as well.

Their plan was ruined. She should run before things got even messier.

A long fingernail touched his lip. "I'm going to let her run around my kingdom, and we'll see what she does. I'm curious what this little faerie thinks she can accomplish. I don't know where she is or where she's staying but...this will be fun. I can't wait to see your face when I kill her."

Donnacha wanted to scream that he'd like to see her try, but he couldn't. Instead, all he could do was lay there as his cell door closed again.

Screaming only in his mind.

ELVA RETURNED to the hill where the buggane had first dropped her off. Her breath came in sharp gasps. She wasn't sure what she was going to do next. He was in a dungeon, barely even alive, and there was nothing more she could do. The trolls had him well and truly. She couldn't walk him out of that cell with so many eyes watching him.

The bushes beyond the hill rustled, and beady red eyes stared out at her. "Well? Did you do it?" the buggane asked as it clambered toward her.

"Do what?" Elva shook her head. "I thought you said you were going home."

"I did. I went home, and now I'm back."

The lumbering bulk of the buggane looked very much like the trolls. Elva could understand how some people might mistake them. But now she knew there was a kindness in the buggane's eyes that wasn't in the vacant expression of the trolls. This creature wanted to help others. She wanted to see stories come to life and live through the happiness of others.

The buggane was trustworthy, where the trolls wouldn't know the meaning of the word.

Elva sat down on the hill, drawing the cloak tighter around her shoulders against the chilly night air. "I don't know what I'm going to do now."

"You could have tossed him over your shoulder and ran?" the buggane suggested, settling down on the ground next to her. "Or maybe you could have gone in with your sword raised, ready to take the heads of all who tried to stop you."

"That only happens in stories. In real life, people who do that don't live longer than a few seconds."

The furred faerie harrumphed. "Well, that makes things a lot more difficult."

Yes, it did. Elva had seen what was within the fortress walls, and it wasn't good. They had Donnacha under constant guard. And if he was always drugged like that, then he wouldn't be able to help her get him out. Which meant she was going to have to figure this out on her own.

Or maybe not. She looked up at the buggane with a calculating look. "How did you know he was in the dungeon?"

The creature shifted awkwardly, scooting a little further away from her. "I just did."

"You were watching me, weren't you?"

"Maybe."

"Well, did you see anything useful then?"

The buggane shrugged. "I saw a few things."

Elva rolled her eyes, then shivered as a gust of wind pushed through the cloak. "All right. Out with it then. I'm welcome to any suggestions, cause I'll be honest, I'm not seeing much here."

"Come here." The buggane held out her arms. "You're cold and I'm not. We'll scheme together while you catch your breath. It's always cold in the troll kingdom."

She didn't want to get any closer to that wet dog smell, but she was very cold. Elva ground her teeth together and snuggled into the fur of the buggane. It was a small price to pay for the warmth that immediately surrounded her.

"Out with it now," Elva said.

"I might have been wandering among the trolls, finding out what I could find out."

"Why?"

"I thought you might need a little help. The faerie princesses in all the stories had some kind of sidekick."

And the buggane thought she was going to be that sidekick. As much as Elva hated the idea of being in some kind of story, she'd admit it was very helpful to have someone else around.

She nodded. "Well, thank you then. If you have an idea, I'm fresh out of them, so I'd certainly be interested in hearing what you have to say."

"Word in the kingdom is that the trolls are having a ball."

"A ball?" Elva lifted a brow and craned her neck to look up at the buggane. "Why?"

"Apparently, the dwarf has gotten into the heads of the royals. They have decided that only a royal wedding would have a ball extravagant enough to make the Seelie Court jealous. They want to have a dance with gowns and all the trappings of normal wedding celebrations."

"Goodness." Elva couldn't imagine what that was going to look like. Trolls in ballgowns? What was the world coming to?'

"That's about what I said, and what the rest of the kingdom is likely saying. Trolls are as likely to enjoy something like that as a buggane." The creature shuddered. "It's a disgusting practice. I don't know how you Seelie faeries do it."

"Sometimes it's fun." She remembered her first ball. How terrified she'd been and how awful it was. The men wanted to dance with her and only her. Elva had been the prettiest and most eligible girl there. Of course, all the other women didn't like that. They'd made the evening a living hell for her.

"I think you need to go to that ball," the buggane forcefully said.

"Why?"

"Balls are always where the prince and princess meet. That's where he'll see you and fall in love all over again. He'll remember why he wanted to marry you and not the troll princess."

No, she wasn't going to listen to that. "Donnacha doesn't want to marry me *or* the troll princess."

"Of course, he wants to marry you. Who wouldn't?"

Her mother had said the same thing when Elva had been looking for a husband. Elva struggled out of the buggane's arms and tried to catch her breath. Anxiety loomed over her like a great shadow. "This is a bad idea. Waltzing into that place is only going to start a fight."

"Not if they don't know who you are." The buggane pulled a sack closer to her, one Elva hadn't realized she'd carried up the hill. "After all, a disguise is also a part of every good story."

Elva watched as the buggane pulled out a glorious swath of smoky gray fabric. Tiny diamonds twinkled like stars throughout the entire thing. It was beautiful in the way the night sky was beautiful. Dangerous, vast, and untouchable.

"Where did you get that?" she asked, reaching out to stroke the beautiful silk.

"I have friends." The buggane's chest puffed up with pride. "But I think you need to wear this."

"They'll never let me in if I'm wearing this."

"They don't have to. You have a cloak. Hide everything, look like a hunchbacked troll wandering in. All you have to do is get an invitation."

"Who's going to give me an invitation?" Elva said with a laugh, letting her hand drop from the beautiful fabric.

"Well, you bribed your way into the dungeon." The buggane grinned. "Bribe your way into the ball."

18

Elva tugged at the edge of her cloak, making sure it covered everything. This was the worst plan she'd ever gone along with. Why had the buggane suggested this? Wandering into the ball, celebrating the wedding of Donnacha and the troll princess, when she was the only person who planned on stopping said wedding?

They were going to find her, and then they were going to destroy her with a single well-placed sword. She'd been far too confident in her abilities and sorely underestimated the number of trolls here. However, this might be her only chance to talk with Donnacha. He might have ideas on how to escape, and that was the first step toward saving him.

She stepped into the garden where she'd first seen the troll princess. It was highly likely the creature would be here again. The buggane said she spent quite a lot of time in the gardens of the castle. Not because she liked gardening or even appreciated the beauty. Apparently, the troll princess liked to step on blooming flowers.

Strange creatures, these trolls. But the buggane had been certain that even now, when the ball was beginning, the troll princess would make her way out here. Just to make herself feel better before it all started.

Elva stuck to the shadows, watching the back door of the castle until it opened up and the troll princess stumbled out. Was she drunk already? It appeared so.

She was covered in little more than a few scraps of glittery fabric. Elva had no idea what it was made of, but it showed far too much of her body. Really, it was just two circles over her flat chest where nipples might be, and a tiny loincloth that shifted a little too much when she moved.

Was this what she thought a wedding dress looked like? The garishly colored fabric wasn't quite bride material. Maybe this was just the unfinished beginning of the final dress. At least, Elva hoped the strange pieces of fabric were just undergarments..

The princess hiccupped, then wandered toward a rose bush. "Stupid flowers," she muttered. "Stupid pretty things thinking they're better than me."

Goodness, she stepped on the flowers because they were more attractive?

Elva took a deep breath and moved forward. "Princess?"

The princess flinched, caught one foot underneath the other, and fell onto her backside. She scrambled away from the sound before her gaze landed on Elva. "Oh, it's just you, the hunchback."

At least Elva knew the cloak really was hiding everything it needed to hide. She tugged the edge closer, hoping it looked like she was embarrassed about the way she looked, and walked closer. "Yes, it is I."

"What do you want?"

That was easier than she thought it would be. Elva cleared her throat. "I have heard the celebration of your wedding to the dwarf will be the grandest event the troll kingdom has ever seen. I would like an invitation."

"Why?"

"To see you in all your splendor, of course."

The troll princess stood, brushing leaves and sticks off her backside. "I think you're a little too interested in my groom."

"I don't know what you're talking about." Maybe the princess wasn't as drunk as Elva thought.

"I think you want him for yourself." The princess stepped closer menacingly. She loomed over Elva and, for a second, Elva thought the gig was up. But then, the princess began to laugh. "Do you really think he'd choose you over me? The hunchback of the troll kingdom? Hardly."

Elva bowed low. "You are right, Your Majesty. I could never compete with your beauty. However, I would still like to see the party. If only for the memories."

That was a little too close to a lie. Though sarcasm did count as a truth, she wasn't sure she wanted to actually see the party. It was a little too much for even her. How was she going to keep herself hidden with that many creatures in close quarters?

The troll princess looked her up and down, then held out her hand. "What do you have for me this time?"

Of course, there was going to have to be a deal. Elva had made enough of them in her life to know this creature would want something more than just a golden apple this time.

She reached behind her into the pack that created the hump on her spine and fished around for what she might find. Though the position must look odd, the troll princess didn't blink an eye. Maybe she thought Elva was pulling something out of her behind, for all she knew.

Her fingers caught on a chain and a clasp. Now, this was something that would convince the troll princess to allow her access easily enough.

Elva withdrew the necklace with a flourish and let the chain dangle from her fingers. "A gift for the most beautiful troll in the wedding."

It was a dainty piece, a thin golden chain and a single bead with an emerald the size of Elva's thumbnail. Still, it somehow managed to look quite simple and beautiful.

She hoped that was something the troll princess would enjoy. Such a thing didn't seem to be her kind of jewelry.

Glancing up, Elva watched the troll's eyes glaze over with want. "It's so shiny."

All right then, trolls were apparently interested in shiny things as well as gold. That was something she'd have to store away in her mind for another time.

Elva shifted her hand, swinging the chain to keep the troll's attention. "And it's yours if you let me into the ball."

"Done." The troll princess lunged forward for the necklace.

Elva pulled it away at the last second. "And a dance with your groom."

"A dance? Why would he want to dance with a hunchback?" She tried to grab the necklace again, only to lean back and stomp when Elva wouldn't give it to her. "You said it was a deal!"

"I didn't. I want a dance with the groom. He can tell me he's not interested himself, but I'd like to at least try without troll guards threatening to kill me."

The troll princess pouted, her lip thrust out, before she finally caved and nodded. "Fine. But I want you to put the necklace on me now."

"It will compliment your outfit wonderfully, Your Majesty."

The troll princess turned around and lifted the scraggly end of her ponytail. Elva couldn't believe the foolish girl. She gave someone she didn't know her neck? How in the world had she not been murdered already?

Elva linked the clasp and let the necklace drop onto the troll's thick neck. The chain was immediately swallowed in the gray rolls, but she could see the emerald just fine when the troll turned around. It was... beautiful? Maybe. It certainly did stand out amongst the gray, like a gemstone deep in a mine.

"It's lovely," she murmured, bowing low.

The princess fingered the stone, then said, "You know, I think I like you, hunchback. Your gifts are always so much better than everyone else's."

Of course, they were. Her gifts were dwarven made. Elva bowed low again. "Thank you, Your Majesty. Anything to please you."

"Those are words I love to hear. Come on then, hunchback. You can come in the back way with me. We'll go back to the ball together. Maybe I'll make you stand next to me for the rest of the night. You certainly make me look far lovelier."

Elva trailed along behind her, praying the cloak would stay in place. The hood over her face was so long, it was highly unlikely anyone would peer into the shadows it created. But if someone saw her, that would be the end of this charade.

The interior of the castle was as unimpressive as she was expecting. There wasn't much here at all, just a blank room carved into the stone and a few tables that had been shoved to the side. No decorations, no carvings, nothing but rough stone and a throne at the far end.

The troll princess strode into the room with her head held high. With good reason, all the other trolls flinched away from her. They created a pathway for her to walk down to her mother.

Elva watched the others and their angry faces. None of them wanted to be here, wearing the strange clothes that didn't fit them. A few of them wore giant collars and nothing else. Some were in full suits splitting at the seams because they'd pulled too hard to try to fit them. The women were in giant gowns that bulged in all the wrong places.

This wasn't anything like a ball in the Seelie Court, and the rest of the troll kingdom knew it. They hated being here, and if she was reading their expressions correctly, they hated the royals for forcing them to be here.

Strange. Elva had heard of quite a few people hating royal families before. She'd been married to one of the worst Seelie

King's in history. But she'd never seen so many people wearing that fact on their sleeves and clearly trying their best to glare daggers into the backs of those people they hated.

The trolls didn't make sense. If anyone in the Seelie Court had been so blatant about their feelings, they would have been beheaded immediately. An investigation would have been launched to see what their family was doing, and then their family would have been likely removed from the history books as well. They would have nothing left because they clearly had wanted to kill the royals.

Did the troll queen and princess not care? Or did they merely not think the others were a threat?

Instead of following the troll princess, Elva melted into the crowd. She listened to conversations when she could, trying to figure out where Donnacha was.

Some of the trolls said he was still getting prettied up, others said they'd already seen him. He wasn't standing with the Troll Queen, so where had they put him?

A band started up, the reedy sound of a flute and twin violins shrieking throughout the ballroom. What in the world was that godawful sound?

Elva forced her hands to remain at her sides so she didn't reach up to cover her ears. Was this the live music? This sound that was equal to a harpy screaming?

The crowd shifted, creating a circle in the center of the room. And there was Donnacha, clutched against the troll princess's chest, feet off the ground. Oh, the poor man, Elva thought. He was going to hate every second of the dance.

She could see it on his face. Every inch of his body was tense, and his face was wrinkled into a frown. She couldn't imagine what the troll princess smelled like that close, but she was certain it was worse than the buggane.

They danced four songs. Four long songs where the troll princess whirled him around as his feet dangled limply.

Donnacha's arms were squeezed down at his side and his neck must have hurt by this point as he desperately had tilted it away from her.

Elva made her way through the crowd when the troll princess finally set him down to pick up a bucket of water. She was apparently trying to quench her thirst, but most of the water poured down her body. An attempt to seduce Donnacha? Or maybe just... Elva didn't want to think about it.

She shifted closer to Donnacha and exaggerated her hunch even more. He stared down at a table where goblets had been set. There were things floating in almost all of them, likely the reason why he wore such an expression of disgust. "May I have this dance, good sir?" She kept her voice quiet and rough so none of the trolls would overhear and question who she was.

"I'm only allowed to dance with the troll princess," he snarled.

"I traded her a rather precious necklace for the opportunity to share your company."

"Then you can dance with her."

Elva stepped closer. "I don't want to dance with her, Donnacha. I want to dance with you."

He froze. She watched the tension in his shoulders disappear. He turned around so she could see him fully, and Elva smiled.

"You're clean," she said. His face was finally free of grime, his hair brushed. Someone had braided his long, dark locks and tangled small metal clasps throughout. The navy blue doublet he wore was an old style, but it was little better than what the rest of the trolls wore. Clearly, the troll princess wanted him to be impressive.

Still, he looked good. She hadn't seen him like this before. He'd always been covered in layers of grime while in the Troll Kingdom or hidden in the shadows at the castle. But this... He really looked like the dwarven noble he was.

Elva smiled and pulled back her hood only enough for him to

see her face but no one else to sneak a peek of her. "Hello, Donnacha."

"You're here," he said, his expression stunned. "How are you here?"

"I made a deal."

"It better have not been too much of a deal. These trolls are dangerous beings to be making deals with."

Elva shook her head and tugged the hood back in place. "I gave her something in return for a dance with you."

"I'm not a very good dancer."

"Well, you'll be happy to know that I am a very good dancer." She held out her hand for him to take. "Come on, Donnacha."

"It's dangerous. They'll figure out who you are."

"All good things are a little bit dangerous."

He reached out for her hand and slid his fingers into hers. The bulge on her back where the rest of her dress was gathered along with the pack, made it difficult for her to straighten. Still, she did her best to help him as he waltzed with her through the crowd to the clamorous music.

"You shouldn't be here," he whispered.

"Neither should you. And yet, we've both found ourselves in this horrible place. Now, work with me to get us both out of here."

Donnacha leaned up and muttered into her ear, "They know you're here."

A chill danced down her spine. "Who?"

"The Troll Queen. She told me right after you left my cell. She saw you while you were visiting me but was going to let you stay just to see what you would do. You have to leave, Elva."

"I'm not leaving you here."

His hand tightened at her waist, tugging her closer. "You have to."

She didn't want to leave him in this depraved place full of creatures who wanted to hurt them both. He didn't deserve that kind of treatment, and he certainly didn't deserve her abandonment.

But she couldn't think of anything else to do. If he didn't want to help her, if the Troll Queen knew she was here, this mission just got impossibly more difficult.

She shook her head. "No. There has to be a way. There's always a way."

He spun her past the troll princess who pointed at them dancing and shouted, "Look at him dance with the ugly hunchback! Isn't she terrible?"

The laughing faces of trolls whirled by her, and it was almost too much to bear. They had taken everything from her, and she hadn't realized it until this instance. Donnacha was a good man. He deserved a life of happiness and respect. Not the future that was building for him here.

"I can't leave you here," she whispered again. "Not this place."

"It won't be so bad. I think they'll probably let me go once they're done with me."

"Not with this plan you built. She thinks you're going to be her husband, and that's a rather lasting position in the troll kingdom."

Donnacha's eyes grew sad, though he tried to smile through the anguish. "I'm sorry, Elva. I wish there was more I could ask of you. I just don't see a way out of this. Not when it would be a fool's errand. We'll both die if we try to escape this. And one of us should live."

All seemed lost in that moment as he stared into her eyes. She couldn't imagine leaving him here. She'd failed so many people in her life, the mere thought of failing him as well made her heart shatter.

What was she going to do? What would the princess in a fairytale do?

Elva smiled then looked into Donnacha's eyes. "Then if they already know I'm here, why am I hiding?"

"What?"

"They're expecting me to be here, Donnacha. I'm not afraid of the Troll Queen or what she can do. We might as well give them the show they've been waiting for."

"I'm not sure that's a good idea."

"I am." She took his hand at her waist and coiled his fingers in the fabric of the cloak. "Dance with me, Donnacha, and let's show them how a real Seelie Court hosts a ball."

"What are you doing?" His eyes widened in shock the moment she spun away from him.

Elva channeled every bit of herself that she used to be, the woman who had walked into a ball and had every eye on her. The first spin took away the cloak. The second and others that followed revealed the beautiful storm cloud of a dress. Gossamer fabric danced down her arms like mist, turning into diamond-studded lightning around her legs.

Elva shook her hair down around her shoulders in curls as golden as wheat. She raised her arms above her head in a pirouette and then slowed her turns until she ended in a graceful curtsey.

The trolls gasped and took steps away from her, as if she were frightening in her beauty. And she was. For the first time in many centuries, Elva felt all the things that Donnacha had seen in her. She could be feminine and fierce at the same time. Soft and strong.

She raised her hand, stepped forward, and then waited until he placed his hand at her waist once more. He looked up into her eyes with all his heart in his gaze.

"You are beautiful," he said. "My warrior woman who smells like wildflowers."

Elva hadn't realized she wanted to hear those words so desperately until he said them. Gods, he was the most perfect man she'd ever met, and she wanted to devour him.

The smile on her face hurt it was so wide. "I'm so tired of listening to this music, my dear."

She lifted her hands and snapped her fingers. The musicians looked around in confusion before looking down at their instruments once more. This time when they picked them up, they played the most stunning symphony the trolls would ever hear in their lifetimes.

"How did you do that?" Donnacha asked.

"Have you ever seen a Tuatha de Danann use magic?"

"Never."

"Good." She leaned down and tugged him closer. "I'm glad I'm your first."

If it hadn't been quite so loud in the ballroom, Elva was certain she would have heard him audibly gulp. The poor man hadn't stood a chance at keeping his heart when they'd had nothing but darkness and shadows between them. Now that he could see her and she was back to her former glory… Well, Elva pitied the man.

An angered shout rocked through the room. "Mummy! She's too pretty to be near my groom. *She's supposed to be an ugly hunchback!"*

The Troll Queen whirled in her armored gown and lifted a hand. "Guards! Apprehend that woman!"

Big words for a creature who refused to dirty her hands with battle.

Elva arched a brow. "Do you trust me, Donnacha?"

"With my life."

"Then dance with me dwarf. Let's see how good I am at magic these days."

Donnacha didn't wait. He tugged her into a waltz, and Elva unleashed all the power she'd held at bay since she became the wife of the Seelie King. She hadn't wanted Fionn to see how powerful she could be because he hadn't wanted her to be stronger than him. Back then, she'd thought men didn't like women who were infinitely *more* than them.

Donnacha had given that back to her. This dwarf who had realized she was worthy no matter what was inside her or what she was capable of. This dwarf who appreciated her abilities just because they were hers and no one else's.

It took only a breath of thought, and they lifted into the air. Waltzing across the tops of the trolls and higher and higher. No one could reach them up here. Though they could still hear the angered shouts, the music was louder and filled their ears with much more pleasant sounds.

"How is this possible?" he asked.

"Faerie magic is like a wish. All you have to do is believe and then...magic happens."

"That's remarkable." He paused, "I had forgotten that."

"It's not really," she said, her cheeks burning with a blush. "But I'm glad you think so."

Donnacha's hand tightened at her waist. "What would we have done if we met like this at a Seelie ball?'

She laughed. "We never would have met at a Seelie ball. The dwarves would have stayed to themselves, and I would have had a hundred Tuatha de Danann jostling for my attention."

"Ah, because you are the most beautiful woman they've ever seen?"

"Because they like to own shiny things, and I am all the rage now that I'm free." She slid her hand up his shoulder and touched his chin. "But I still would have seen you from across the room. Even in all this splendor, you still carry something of the mountain with you."

"Do I?"

"Something in the set of your jaw, the stubbornness there, or maybe it's the deep blue of mountain lakes in your eyes."

Donnacha twirled her in a circle, raising his arm for her to dip under before bringing her back to his chest. "I never would have thought a warrior woman could be a poet."

"And why not?"

"You're a woman of action, not of words."

She looked at him with all the softness inside her, all the kindness that came pouring out because he had fixed her. "Words abandoned me for a while. They fled from my head and dripped off my tongue in bitter droplets, but you gave them back to me. You reminded me that rosewater is not something to be afraid of, even in myself. I don't have to frighten people away. By doing that, all I've done is miss out on meeting more people like you."

"I'm glad I could give you that." He rubbed her back. "It's a shame I couldn't see you put that to good use."

"Are you really giving up then?"

He nodded. "I am. And you should, too. Leave this cursed place. Go on all the adventures you thought you would and remember me while you're there."

Elva shook her head. "I'm not going to toss your ashes off the cliffs, Donnacha. You aren't dead yet, and that means I can still save you."

"You're a stubborn woman."

"Yes, I am."

He sighed in anger and then finally nodded. "Fine. Come to me one last time. We'll figure it out."

"I will."

"How are you going to get out of this ballroom now that everyone knows you're here?"

Relief flooded her chest. He hadn't given up just yet, which meant neither would she. There was a chance now, and that was all she needed.

Elva tucked a hand behind his neck. "Dip me and then kiss me, dwarf."

"Yes ma'am."

He stopped them in a grand twirl, dipped her with his hands holding her close to his heart. Donnacha hesitated for a brief moment when she heard the enraged scream of the troll princess.

"I think I might love you," he whispered the moment before he kissed her.

And it was a kiss to end all kisses. She'd never forget the way he devoured her lips and poured secrets into her soul. He gave her everything he was. The promise of a future, the salty taste of hope, and the cool salve knowing he believed in her.

Elva cupped his jaw and gave him everything she was back. The hope that they would see another life together because she had traveled across the realms to find him and wasn't letting him go just yet.

When it was finished, she licked her lips and looked up into his eyes. "Stay alive, Donnacha. I will come for you."

"Anything for you."

Elva flexed her power one last time. The spell would set him back on the ground gently, and it made her melt from his arms and appear on the hill beyond the castle once more. Here, she would plan her attack.

She would get him back.

19

Elva breathed out a sigh that created mist in the cold morning air. This was her last chance. She focused her attentions on what could save Donnacha, and it had to be the best deal she'd made yet with the troll princess.

Shuffling footsteps approached her from the bottom of the hill. "Faerie?"

The buggane was still here. She'd been so enchanted by the story Elva had told her on she had repeated it when they met again. The dress had worked, well, sort of. She'd been so defeated that even the magic of the evening and the faces of the disappointed trolls hadn't been enough to make her happy.

Elva turned. "Hello, buggane."

"Is there anything else I can do?"

Not really. There was so much happening that she couldn't think. There was only one more deal to make, and then she feared Donnacha would really give up. Elva brushed her hair away from her face and nodded. "Return home, buggane. See if you can find the king of the dwarves and tell him to race here with an army if possible. There might need to be a war to get him out."

"But the king didn't want that."

"You may tell him I am concerned I will fail. That both Donnacha and I might be caught, and all will be lost."

"You can't think like that, faerie princess. Stories like these always end happily."

She wasn't so sure this was a fairytale after all. With everything they'd suffered through, with everything they'd survived, she had a feeling this would end a different way.

Elva shook her head. "Just go. Let him know that he is needed. Whether we succeed or not, I don't think the journey will be easy for either of us to make."

The buggane finally nodded and trudged back down the hill. Elva watched the furry beast until she disappeared into the undergrowth. Somehow, the strange creature had become rather dear to Elva. She wasn't sure how that happened, or when.

Elva had never made friends easily, even when she didn't have the weight of her own disappointment riding on her shoulders.

Back when she was a spoiled brat, no one had wanted to hear what she had to say. No one other than Bran, and then he'd married her sister, so what did that really say? She had thoughts in her head, but no one really wanted to hear those thoughts. They wanted to look at her, to find her pretty, but never for her to open her mouth.

Then, she'd taken back her life in a grasp that was used to heft a sword, to swing it at those who denied her rights. Unfortunately, that had brought about even less friends. No one wanted to be seen with the faerie princess who had gotten herself involved with less than acceptable hobbies.

The buggane had seen through that. She'd smiled when Elva didn't think she knew how to smile anymore. She'd opened her arms and created a warm haven when Elva was cold, without anyone asking her to. And most importantly, the buggane believed in her.

Elva didn't know what to do with that.

No one had ever believed in her so easily before, other than Donnacha, who was just as much a mystery as the buggane.

Who were these faeries who trusted so easily? And how did they do it?

She turned back toward the castle and wondered if the Troll Queen could see her even now. The queen hadn't reacted at all when she'd revealed herself. Did the creature have someone watching her?

Elva wondered if it was truly because the woman had such confidence that she didn't care if Elva was there. If she really thought that no one could defeat her.

The pack weighed heavy on Elva's spine. It almost felt as though it were getting heavier with every step toward the castle. Furrowing her brows in confusion, she reached behind her and closed her fingers on the hilt of what was clearly a sword. What magic was this? Was this the next item she was supposed to give the troll princess?

Flowers tainted the air with the most beautiful of scents. Petals that had fallen to the ground crunched under her feet as she made her way toward a bench to wait for the troll princess.

The sun had come out in a rare moment of warmth for the troll kingdom. Elva desperately wanted to feel the heat on her face, so she supposed it wouldn't be the end of the world if she tilted back her head and closed her eyes. The hood fell from covering her face, and she left it at her shoulders. They already knew who she was. Even the troll princess wasn't so foolish that she would mistake the hunchback for anything other than faerie now.

The door to the castle slammed open, and the troll princess stomped toward her. "*You!*"

Elva kept her head tilted back. She carefully shifted the pack from her shoulders, however, and let it fall to the ground at her feet. "Yes, me."

"Do you know how much you embarrassed me? Mother yelled at me all night!"

"I'm sure she did."

"You made it seem like you were a hunchback! Not..." The troll princess waited until Elva opened her eyes and looked at her, then waved up and down. "This."

"A faerie?"

"You're more than just a faerie. You're from the Seelie Court!"

"Yes, I am." And for the first time in her life, she was proud to say that. She didn't want to hide who she was or where she came from. She wanted the troll princess to know that a true thing of beauty sat before her, and she should be intimidated by that fact.

The troll princess faltered in her anger, staring into Elva's gaze. "But why?"

"Why what?"

"Why did you lie to me? Or make it seem like you weren't who you were? You can't possibly be interested in a dwarf." The troll spat the last word like it left a bitter taste in her mouth.

"You're interested in the dwarf."

"I only want him because he will make my children strong. You don't want to have children. Seelie faeries never do. So why are you interested in him?"

Elva thought about misleading the troll again. She could convince her there was something else going on, that Donnacha owed her a beautiful trinket or he should have given her something in the form of a deal. But she didn't want to lie anymore. "He makes me feel like a person again."

The troll princess shook her head in confusion. "I don't understand."

"Neither do I really, but then again, men are difficult to understand." If she had understood their kind a long time ago, then she might have stayed out of the mess of her life.

They stared at each other in silence for a little while. Elva couldn't hazard a guess at what was going through the troll princess's mind. She was a dim-witted creature, although Elva was certain there was something else underneath the fabric of this creature's being. The troll princess wanted people to think she was foolish. In Elva's experience, that was rarely the case with women like that.

Finally, the troll princess blew out a breath and raised her arms in the air. "Fine then. What do you want this time?"

"I want to make another deal."

"For what?"

"A little time with the dwarf. Yet again."

The troll princess crossed her arms, and Elva saw there was a glint of emerald still at her throat. "I'm just going to put him to sleep again. You realize this, yes?"

"Even if you do, it was worth the trade."

"To sit and stare at a sleeping man? You'll have to excuse me when I say I don't believe that at all."

So she was a little more intelligent than she let the rest of them believe. Elva pitied this creature who had more between her ears than just the thoughts of a foolish child. "What do you want? Let me ask this first before I say anything else. What do you want out of life, Troll Princess?"

The other woman hesitated. Her eyes narrowed, and she stared at Elva with a calculating look that didn't go with her personality in the slightest. "Why do you ask?"

"I wonder if this is all your mother's plan, and not yours at all. To fall in love with a dwarf is a difficult thing. I know this to be true. I don't see you as someone who wants to be a mother yet, so I don't think you want him for a child. Why is he here? Why are you here?"

"I want to make my mother proud." But her eyes slanted to the side when she said it.

"That's what everyone says you should want, I'm sure. But what do *you* want, Troll Princess?"

When the troll princess opened her mouth, there was something else in her words. Some hint of light and desire and truth that Elva hadn't heard before. For a moment, Elva thought she had managed to convince the creature to tell the truth.

Then it disappeared. Like a mask had fallen over her face, the troll princess glowered and then stamped her foot. "Just give me what you have in your pack!"

Fine. If that was the game they were going to play, then Elva would make sure she played her part. She reached into the pack and drew out the gleaming golden sword.

The hilt was a wolf swallowing the blade, and she recognized this fake for what it tried so desperately to mimic. The Sword of Nuada. The legendary blade that could make an army stop in its tracks and men fall to their knees to be beheaded without complaint.

She swallowed hard then looked at the troll princess whose mouth had fallen open. "Do you know what this sword is?"

"Nuada's blade," the troll princess said with awe.

If Elva didn't correct the other woman, it wasn't technically a lie. So she didn't.

The troll princess reached out for the sword and took it. A shiver traveled down Elva's spine at the sight. She shouldn't have given this creature a sword, not when she already had everyone else under her heel. But the troll princess didn't swing it at Elva. Instead, she hefted it in her hands and let the tip touch the ground.

"It's beautiful," the troll princess whispered. "I never thought to see it in my lifetime."

"Neither had I."

"Why would you give me something so precious? Just to see a dwarf?"

Elva shrugged. "He's more important to me than a sword."

"I don't understand that thought," the troll princess replied, her hands curling more comfortably around the hilt. "I've never thought so highly of someone that I would give up so many precious things."

"They're just objects. Emotions can't be replaced with physicals things. It's like trying to replace the song of a bird with a bird itself. Without the music, the bird is just another bird."

Again, the troll shook her head. "I still don't understand."

"The sword is gifted for a night with the dwarf and the assurance that your mother will not appear again."

"Again?" The troll didn't look at her, though.

"I know you told her that I was going to see the dwarf. She saw me, and that's why your mother had any idea I was here. I want a few moments alone with the dwarf, whether he's awake or not. With the assurance that no one will disturb us."

The troll princess chewed on her lip. "There will be guards."

"No guards."

"I'm not capable of magic. Mother has requested the dwarf be watched at all times with guards. He's crafty."

"So am I. I give you my solemn vow. If you take the guards away, I will not break him out of that prison. We wouldn't get far anyway. Move the guards to the front of the dungeon for all I care, but I will have some time alone with him."

Elva watched the troll princess think. Did the creature realize all her thoughts played across her face? She could see the inner battle as she thought about how she'd do it and the rage her mother would have if she ever found out.

Just when she thought the troll princess had settled on a decision she wouldn't like, Elva leaned forward to reach for the blade. "If you can't do it, I'll take the sword back."

The troll princess flinched away from her, taking the sword with her. "No, I want the legendary blade."

"Then you have to do what I've asked."

"Fine."

Elva arched a delicate brow. "Then it's a deal?"

The troll princess hesitated only for a moment before she

nodded. "It's a deal. Come back tomorrow night, late in the evening when the sun has set. The dungeon will be unlocked and the guards distracted. You should be able to slip in easily enough. They won't notice you. You're too little."

Little? That was something Elva had never been called before. But she nodded and pulled the hood of her cloak low over her face. "You have yourself a deal, Troll Princess."

"I better not get in trouble for this."

UNDER THE COVER OF NIGHT, Elva made her way into the dungeon. The guards were gone as the troll princess had said, but she wasn't confident there wouldn't be trolls lurking in the shadows ready to grab her. The trolls had proven themselves to be far more dangerous than she'd ever given them credit for.

She'd wrapped her feet in fabric from her gown to muffle her footsteps. The dress she'd worn to the ball was soft and thin, perfect to quiet the sound, although she was sad to rip it. Apparently, she was more like her mother. That woman hadn't ever wanted to destroy beautiful things either.

Carefully, Elva slid along the wall. She kept her gaze on the moving shadows and held her breath in case it was too loud.

No one moved toward her. No one launched themselves out of the darkness to grab her and drag her to another cell. Which meant the troll princess had somehow kept her word. Strange.

Elva remembered which cell was his. It wasn't easy to forget, although there were plenty of interesting things happening in the other cells.

One of the captured trolls groaned as she passed by. The male, or at least she thought it was a male, had stuck himself to the wall in hopes he might live a little longer. She wanted to tell him not to be afraid of the dying light in his soul. There was more for him in the afterlife than staying here, lingering in the darkness of the cells and the damp wet air.

They wouldn't listen to her anyway. The trolls didn't believe in the Seelie Court's myths of what death was like. They, like the Unseelie Court, didn't believe faeries had souls.

Maybe they were right, but she didn't want to find out until the last second of her life when everything faded from view.

She touched her fingers to the cold bars of the cell where Donnacha laid on his cot. Had she really put him to sleep again? That would put a wrench in her plans. She'd wanted to speak with him, to figure out what they were going to do.

Pulling the bars open, she moved into the cell with a whisper of shifting fabric.

"Donnacha?" she asked. "Are you awake?"

His fingers twitched.

Elva moved closer to him, pulling off her cloak and laying it over his body that was somehow dirty already. "I'm sorry, dwarf. I know this isn't the easiest thing you've ever suffered through. But I do think we'll be able to figure out a plan."

His eyes opened, although it was a struggle. He looked at her with panic and desperation.

She wouldn't have that.

Elva touched her fingers to his cheek and smiled as brightly as she could muster. "I'll tell you everything. And by the time I'm done, the poison will have worn off. Don't worry, Donnacha, everything is going to be all right."

She told him everything she'd done with the troll princess, starting from the beginning. If anyone would know what to do, it was Donnacha. He let his eyes drift shut as she spoke, but she knew he was listening.

Halfway through the tale, he slowly shifted his hand across the cot and then covered hers with the warmth of his. How did he manage to always make her stomach clench? Just from a small movement, and it wasn't like he'd done much.

Elva stumbled over her words. He couldn't know that meant so much to her, could he? Did he know his support was the only thing keeping her from flying apart into a thousand pieces?

She'd guessed the poison's longevity correctly. By the time she told him about the sword, Donnacha moved to sit up on the cot. He shook his hands to get the feeling back in them.

"A sword?" he said with a grin. "Was that really the best idea?"

"It didn't seem like it at the time. But your cousin gave me this pack and, thus far, it's created items she can't say no to."

"It wasn't really the sword of Nuada, was it?"

She gave him an unimpressed look. "Do you think I'd give something of that power to a troll?"

"I'm just curious because Angus did have that particular item in his possession for a very long time. He's kept it secret, and I highly doubt he'd use it for you, but the man has surprised me before."

Yet again, Elva felt herself tongue-tied. Spluttering, she managed, "Your cousin had the sword of Nuada? The sword everyone in both courts has been searching for? For centuries?"

"Well, Angus isn't centuries old, so it wasn't always in his possession. I think his father was the one who originally found it, but don't tell the dwarf king I was the one who told you that. He thinks it's a good story to tell pretty women." He stared at her with sudden heat. "He didn't try to woo you, did he?"

Elva had to cover her mouth so she didn't bark out laughter. "What?"

"You're his type. You can tell me if he tried something. I'll just break his arm for it when I see him next."

"He didn't try anything," she said with a muffled giggle. "What is it with you dwarves? Are all of you interested in Seelie faeries?"

Donnacha reached out and caught a golden curl between his fingers. He rubbed the silken lock while giving her a stare that made her fists clench. "No, we're not all that interested in Seelie faeries. I think it's just you, Elva."

They weren't pretty words, not really, but somehow they meant all the more. "I was once known as the most beautiful woman in the Seelie court."

"No," he shook his head, dropping the curl to cup his hand around the back of her neck. "It isn't that. It's your confidence, your strength, your ability to continue on in the face of even a troll kingdom. I didn't think it was possible anyone like you existed, and yet, here you are."

His breath fanned across her face. "Here I am, dwarf. Now, what are you going to do with me?"

He shuddered. "So much that I cannot do in a dungeon."

"I've never minded a little dirt."

"Well, I do." Instead of kissing her as she desperately wanted him to, Donnacha leaned up and pressed a kiss to her brow. "You deserve at least something comfortable for our first time."

"First time?" She couldn't help the goosebumps that rose on her arms just from his touch. The idea of sleeping with him, making love or whatever romantic thing people called it these days, wasn't...awful.

When had that happened? The idea of someone touching her had made her shudder in fear, but now the idea of actually allowing him access to her body didn't make her ill.

She'd tried once with another person. She'd thought that if she pushed herself and just *did it,* then she'd get over the fear. Unfortunately, that hadn't happened. The moment the man touched her breast, she'd vomited all over him.

With Donnacha, however, the idea of it wasn't so bad. She didn't think he would rush her or focus on himself so much that he lost sight of her fear. She thought, maybe, he'd listen to her.

Donnacha's lips shifted into a sad smile, and he pulled back. "I don't think you're ready yet, anyway."

"I think I might be."

"Might be isn't going to cut it for me, darling. I want you to know down to your bones that you want me. And that's okay if you're not ready yet. I will wait for you until I know for certain you aren't pushing yourself to do something that will only make things worse. You mean a lot to me, Elva. I can't even explain why or how much, but I don't want to ruin things just because I desperately want to touch you."

She sighed in happiness. This man wasn't trying to make her forget the things that had happened. Instead, he wanted to dull the blade of the memories until they didn't slice at her soul anymore.

Elva leaned forward and pressed her cheek against his. "What are we going to do?"

"The princess didn't tell you the wedding is tomorrow, did she?"

Elva shook her head.

"Then here's the plan. You gave her a legendary sword, or at least one she believes to be legendary. I'm going to tell her that the Seelie Court only allows a man to marry the strongest fighter in the room. She has to battle you for me."

That wouldn't be so hard. She could fight a troll. "All right."

"That easy? You want to fight a troll for me?"

She pulled back so he could see the fierce expression on her face. "If you want to me to fight an entire kingdom of trolls to get you out of here, I would do it. I'm not afraid, Donnacha. Let her fight me and see what it is really like to battle with a warrior."

He gave her an equally feral grin. "So be it. Let the battle begin."

20

Elva held the cloak against her face and hoped none of the trolls surrounding her would recognize the hunchbacked figure as the faerie princess who had made such waves at the ball. The crowd was enough to hide her, and many were wearing cloaks to stop the rain from pouring down onto them. She'd stood in line with the others for hours, waiting to get into the castle.

The wedding was today. Finally, after all this time, she was going to get him out of this place or die trying. Considering the size of the trolls around her, Elva feared that she was chasing death. But it was worth it. If she succeeded.

The crowd moved forward the last step and into the castle she went. Elva weaved through the waiting figures. She was much smaller than the other trolls. Perhaps they thought she was a child because most of them moved aside for her the moment she slipped by.

Or perhaps none of them wanted to stand in the front where the wedding had begun.

The troll princess stood next to Donnacha on a dais in a garish white dress that flounced around her. It floated around her waist, held up by obvious threads connected to her head where her meager hair had been wrapped in a small bun.

The Troll Queen stood in front of them, holding up a rather worn and dusty book that might have once been used for a wedding. Elva recognized the golden letters on the front. Faerie language, and ones only the Tuatha de Danann could read. Which clearly meant whatever the queen was saying were not actual wedding vows that would bind a faerie to another.

Donnacha was wearing the same suit he'd worn at the ball. They must not have had anything else to give him.

His eyes darted through the room every now and then. She watched them shift until he finally caught sight of her. The tension in his shoulders eased a little, then he nodded at her.

Clearing his throat, Donnacha interrupted the proceedings. "There is one last thing, your majesties."

The Troll Queen stopped mid-sentence and narrowed her eyes on him. "We don't have time for that, I'm afraid."

"We must. There's a tradition amongst the dwarves that the bride must fight for her husband."

"Fight?" The troll princess placed a hand on her hip and shook the bun on top of her head. "I'm not fighting anyone for you. I already won you, fair and square."

"It's not fighting *for* me, your majesty. It's merely tradition. Of course, the more powerful an opponent you fight, the more renowned you are throughout the dwarven kingdom."

The Troll Queen threw her head back and laughed. "You haven't given up yet? Do you really think I'm going to let my daughter fight someone of your choosing? Absolutely not. Let's get on with this. We've already catered to your desires far more than we should have."

Donnacha shrugged. "Fine. We can be married in the eyes of the Seelie Court, but the dwarves will never consider us married. They will come for me."

Again, the Troll Queen looked unimpressed. "Let them come. I've never been afraid of a dwarf."

"You should be," Donnacha said, his shoulders squaring as he drew himself up to his peak height. "They will come for me. They will fight, and your kingdom will never have peace unless you do this."

"I don't care. Trolls enjoy fighting, or have you forgotten that?"

"The dwarves do as well. And we have forges that can make blades unheard of before, blades that could cleave the head off any troll."

The Troll Queen chuckled. "You aren't scaring me, Donnacha. I'm not interested in your little games. We'll proceed."

"I won't."

"I don't care if you're married to my daughter or not. If you refuse to proceed with this, that's fine. You're still her gift, and she can still do with you as she pleases."

For a moment, Elva thought they'd lost all control over the situation. If the Troll Queen didn't fall for this, then everything had been for nothing. He was going to have to stay here because, realistically, she couldn't fight all the trolls in this room.

They had failed.

But then, the troll princess stepped closer to her mother and interrupted their argument. "Mother, I don't mind fighting someone."

"You have never been trained how to fight. Step down, child."

"No. Mother, I want to do this. I want to prove to him and his people that I am a worthy woman for this marriage."

"What?" The Troll Queen tilted her head to the side and eyed her only child up and down. "What are you saying?"

The creature next to her gasped in shock. Elva lifted a hand and pressed it to her mouth to mimic the surprise of the crowd. Were they really so interested in this? The trolls liked to fight. The queen had said that herself. Why would they care if the princess was the same as the rest of them?

Why wouldn't they have taught her how to fight?

"I'm not a child anymore, Mother," the troll princess claimed. She gestured for her maid servant, who brought over a wrapped blade.

Elva was certain it was the one she'd given her. The one that would give her so much false hope, have her jump into battle without realizing she was going to lose.

The troll princess unwrapped the sword and turned toward the crowd with it lifted above her head. All around her, trolls erupted into cries of shock and pleasure. The sword of Nuada was finally theirs. The sword that could bring down an army without ever having to fight.

The Troll Queen stepped forward, her brows furrowed and her hands reaching for the sword. "Where did you get that, my daughter?"

"It doesn't matter! Don't you see? I don't mind fighting anyone who wants to challenge me for his hand. It will hardly be a fight."

This was her moment. All she had to do was make a grand entrance, and then everything would go back to plan. Elva hesitated a brief moment, letting the Troll Queen think.

The royal woman wasn't a fool. She knew someone had given her daughter that blade, and she likely didn't think it was for a good reason. The troll queen was a thinker where the rest of her people were creatures of action.

But Elva couldn't give her any more time to think.

"I'll fight you!" she called out, stepping from the crowd and letting her cloak drop to the floor. "Gladly."

She'd worn her own clothing this time. Leather pants, a leather chest plate that would protect her from human warriors, although not likely from a troll. She'd braided her hair back from her face to make sure it didn't get into her eyes. The sword at her side tapped her thigh as she walked, a reminder that Scáthach was still with her even now.

The troll princess's eyes found her. The grin that spread across her face was one of someone who was far too confident. "I've been waiting to fight you since the first moment you walked into this kingdom."

Elva strode forward. If she wanted a fight, then she would get one that would rock her world. The princess wasn't giving her enough credit. But then again, the princess had never tried to find out who she was.

The queen, however, knew exactly who Elva was. She stepped in front of her daughter and shook her head. "Was this your plan all along then, faerie?"

"What plan?" Elva pretended not to know what the troll asked.

"To fight my daughter? To destroy the bloodline of the trolls and insert yourself here in our kingdom?"

Elva smiled. "I don't want your kingdom. If I left the Seelie King, if I chose not to be his queen, then what makes you think I'd want this pathetic excuse for a kingdom?"

"How dare you?" The Troll Queen stepped forward menacingly. "You've outstayed your welcome, Seelie. I'll remove you myself."

She reached down at her side and touched the sword. It had proven to be a good blade thus far, although she was a little concerned a human-made weapon wouldn't be able to slice through troll flesh. Their skin wasn't just rocklike in appearance, but as hard as stone as well.

The troll queen would be a difficult person to fight. She had years of experience and wasn't going to let her win. The queen had likely fought in more battles than Elva could imagine. Their people had always been a warring community in the legends, and this queen had been their ruler for centuries.

Just as the queen stepped forward, her daughter lunged and caught her shoulder. "Mother, no! She's mine."

"You don't know how to use that sword."

"Yes, I do!" The troll princess pointed it at Elva and said, "I want to fight you."

"Then we will do so as only Seelie Court fights can be done." Elva tightened her grip on the sword and widened her stance. "No one else will interfere. Once you agree to fight me, once you step foot on the floor here, then it's just you and me."

The Troll Queen shook her daughter off. "I forbid it."

"Mother!" The troll princess started walking down the stairs. "I am not a child anymore. You cannot control me much longer. This is my decision. And I want to fight."

Only then did the Troll Queen step back. If Elva didn't know any better, she would think the creature was actually angry. Not worried, not thinking that her daughter might lose, but truly angry that her child would defy her.

What mother wouldn't care at all that her child was going to die? And she had to know the troll princess was no match for Elva. Which meant she understood the troll princess was taking her own life in her hands and didn't care other than her child had disagreed with her.

The troll queen sighed and waved in Elva's direction. "Fine then. Fight her and see what happens. I can't teach you everything."

This felt very much like a trap. Elva looked over at Donnacha, who shook his head. He didn't know what was going on either.

She licked her lips and drew her sword. The troll princess left the stairs and strode toward her. All the other trolls shifted, creating a large opening in the middle of the great hall where they would fight.

Was this going to end up another situation where Elva underestimated the trolls? Were they lying that the troll princes didn't know how to fight?

Though that might not be the true sword of Nuada, it was still a sharp dwarven-made blade. She'd never say it out loud, but dwarven blades were dangerous. They knew how to fight even if the wielder wasn't the best warrior. Now if the troll princess was lying and did know how to fight, this could turn on Elva easily.

She wasn't going to underestimate her opponent any longer. She was going to fight this troll princess as though she were sent from Scáthach herself. Then and only then was Elva sure to win.

The troll princess lifted the blade up imperiously and said, "Kneel faerie."

"No."

The princess frowned. "I said kneel."

"I have no intention of doing that." Elva hefted her sword higher. "Lift your blade. I'm not going to kill you if you aren't even attacking me."

True fear lit in the princess's eyes. She shook the sword as if by doing so she might make it work. "Why aren't you doing whatever I want? Is it broken?"

Elva shook her head and moved to slowly circle the princess. "Did you really think I would give you the real sword of Nuada?"

"But faeries can't lie. You said this was the sword of Nuada!"

"No. You were the one who said that. I just didn't correct you."

The troll princess stamped her foot. "But that's not fair! I would never have agreed to fight you if I had known this wasn't the legendary sword. I'm going back up there and I'm going to marry that dwarf. You cheated!"

When she moved toward the stairs, Elva stepped in front of her. The torchlight reflected on her sword, dancing down the surface until it looked like her blade was on fire. "No, you aren't."

"You cheated," the troll princess hissed.

"I did no such thing. I simply didn't correct you. You already made the deal—no one steps foot into the fight to help you, and you can't get out. Lift your sword, princess."

"I don't want to," the troll princess whined the words so they sounded like nails scratching down stone.

Elva's lips twisted into a dark smile. "I didn't want to lose the dwarf, but you took him anyway. Now, I'm going to fight you whether you want to fight or not."

The troll princess's eyes bulged and, for a moment, Elva

thought she might run. Her eyes flicked to the crowd in a desperate attempt to find a way out. But the crowd began to close in around them.

Almost as if they wanted to see their princess die.

Elva looked around at the angry expressions of the trolls and realized they truly hated the royals. Every single person here was staring at the princess with complete and utter rage. They wanted to see her die. They wanted to watch her fight even though they knew she was going to fail because she hadn't been trained.

What kind of creatures were these beings? How had they no compassion?

She shook her head. Once she left this kingdom for good, she was never coming back here. These creatures were toxic.

"Come on, princess," she said again, "lift your sword."

The troll princess looked down at the golden blade in her hand. For a moment, Elva had a flicker of doubt. Perhaps this creature knew how to fight. Maybe this was all one great game to force Elva into a death match that wasn't going to end well.

The thought didn't last long.

With a weak cry, the troll princess lifted the sword over her head and charged forward. She was clearly a novice. She left her entire torso open for attack when Elva was so much smaller than her.

A simple shift would have gutted the princess immediately, but Elva didn't want to win like that. She wanted the troll princess to have at least a modicum of respect when she was finally bested.

Twisting, Elva let the troll princess race past her. The troll fell into the steps, sword clattering as it hit the ground. To her credit, she pushed herself back to standing and whirled rather quickly. For such a large creature, she could move.

Elva kept her sword at her side this time. "Come on," she said. "You can do better than that. Don't hold your sword over your head."

The troll princess didn't listen. She charged like a bull,

although the sword was held straight in front of her. Again, a horrible way to attack anyone. Elva could have sliced through her throat without question if she had wanted to do that.

Shaking her head, she sidestepped again. The troll princess hit the crowd this time. They caught her in their arms and tossed her back toward Elva so forcefully that she might have been toppled if she hadn't expected the others' movement.

Elva had set herself in the world of the warrior. She didn't feel emotions, only calculating steps to predict what the troll princess would do next. But if she would have allowed herself to feel something in that moment, it would have been sadness.

The troll princess was already breathing hard. Her lungs worked to drag in any air that might assist her. Sweat slicked her brow and palms, making it difficult for her to hold onto the hilt of the sword. This wasn't a creature who was meant to fight for her life.

She truly was just a child.

It was time to end this. She had no interest in baiting this child any longer, but she was also angry the trolls didn't care this woman was about to die. They didn't care she was their princess. They didn't care her life was ending. What kind of creatures where these?

White hot anger flowed through her veins. In a quick jab, she sank her blade through the back of the troll princess's knee. The troll gave out a surprised cry and fell to her knees. Just where Elva wanted her.

Pivoting, Elva stepped behind her equally as fast, pressed the blade against the princess's throat, and held her still by the hair.

"Don't move," she growled.

"Please don't kill me. Please, I don't want to die."

And Elva didn't want to kill her. She didn't want to kill anyone, but that decision was entirely up to the queen who stared down at them with blank eyes.

Elva met her gaze and nodded down at the daughter she held

very still. "The option is yours, queen. Let the dwarf go, and I'll let your daughter live."

The Troll Queen shrugged. "I've never been particularly fond of this offspring I've created. There's no need for me to keep her alive when I have a dwarf here who can give me another child. Kill her. I don't really care."

The troll princess choked out a cry.

What kind of mother didn't care if their own daughter died? Then again, what kind of mother sold her only child off to an abusive king who wanted nothing more than to put her on a pedestal for all to see?

Anger at all heartless mothers made Elva see spots. "Are you really that cold?"

"What about trolls makes you think we have hearts?" The queen gestured toward her daughter. "Do you think she wouldn't kill me given the chance? She's tried to poison me for years, but she's not smart enough to trick me. Any of the trolls here would overthrow us both if they had the opportunity. You are not in a kingdom of creatures who care at all about death. It's just a way to more power."

"This is your child."

"And I can make more." The Troll Queen shrugged. "It'll take a little time. I'm sure your dwarf will make it difficult for me, but the men always break eventually."

Elva shook her head, pressing the blade against the troll princess's throat even harder. She was surprised to feel it slice through the bark-like texture. When a bead of blood rolled down the princess's throat, she whimpered for her mother to help.

"One last chance," Elva growled. "One last chance to be a good person for once in your life, to choose your daughter's life above your own."

"Or what?" The queen burst into laughter and opened her arms wide. "If you kill my daughter, then I will order every troll in this hall to kill you. They will destroy you, crack your head upon the stone floor, and bring me a goblet of your blood to drink. You have no other opportunity, faerie princess. Beauty will only get you so far after all."

Elva smiled then. She smiled so brightly it lit up the hall with her happiness. "Then I guess we have to kill you first."

"And how are you going to do that?"

"Oh, I'm not going to," Elva replied. "I was just the distraction."

A shadow behind the queen burst into movement. A blade, dwarven-made as only the dwarves knew how to create a sword that could cut through stone, sliced through the air. The queen's eyes widened as the sword touched her shoulder, sliced through her torso, and exited out the other side.

She had a moment to let out a quiet sound of surprise before the top half of her body slid one way, and the other half slid the other.

The falling remains of the queen revealed the dwarf standing behind her, blade now pointed at the ground. Angus grinned at Elva. "You called?"

"I didn't think you'd have such impeccable timing," she replied.

"A dwarf is never late."

Elva tensed as the trolls around her finally registered what had happened. She lifted her voice above the shouts and concerned words. "Trolls!"

The noise stilled as the others stared at her.

"I hold your last remaining royal with my blade. You will allow us to leave this place unharmed, or I will kill her."

The troll nearest to her snorted. He wore the stone armor of the guards, but he wasn't one she recognized. How many of these creatures were there? "We don't care if you kill her."

"What?" Elva let the question fall from her lips, limp and confused.

The troll princess whimpered. "Mother? Is she dead? Whatever am I going to do?"

Elva felt her chest clench in pain for the poor creature who now mourned her mother. Although she had been a bad mother, she was still the one who had given the princess life. "I'm sorry it came to this."

The troll who had originally spoken, the one she assumed was a guard, shook his head. "She doesn't care the queen's dead any more than the rest of us."

Elva shifted her grip on the princess's hair. "She sure seems to care."

The princess let go of the ruse and sighed when the troll guard stared at her severely. "Fine. No, I don't care that she's gone. The old bitch had it coming."

Elva didn't understand what was going on. This should have been a climactic moment where the trolls rose up in revenge for their queen. Instead, they were already exiting the great hall, murmuring about how that had been the most exciting wedding they'd seen in a while.

Slowly, Elva released the troll princess.

The creature stood, shook herself off, and then pointed at her leg. "That really hurt."

"I'm sure it did. Care to explain what's happening?"

"The fun's over. Now all the trolls will go home, and I'll figure out what I want to do next." The troll princess limped toward the body of her mother. "First, I want to see if she was carrying anything interesting."

"You're—" Elva paused. "Are you looting the body of your mother?"

"Why not?"

As the troll princess rummaged through her mother's pockets, hands quickly becoming red with blood, Elva stepped toward Donnacha. "And...do you want to force this marriage?"

"You won him fair and square. You can have him."

Elva looked at Donnacha, so close she could touch him, and wondered if she was dreaming. "Is this really happening?"

Angus strode up to them, wiping his sword clean. "Damned

trolls. No loyalty among any of them. They just want to see the world fighting, and then when the fight's done, they go back to their homes. Cowards, the lot of them."

"Angus," Donnacha said, reaching for his cousin and tugging him into a tight hug. "It's good to see you."

"The element of surprise always works, don't you think?"

"Worked surprisingly well."

"The queen didn't see it coming."

The two of them laughed, and Elva stared at them in shock. She couldn't process what was happening. The high of battle still running in her veins, she clapped her hands together in a great crack that got their attention. "If you could have broken the deal by killing the queen all this time, why did you send me here?" Elva asked.

Angus shrugged. "I needed you to stall everyone. Donnacha could do that a bit, I was certain of it, but the Troll Queen has never been afraid of men. A woman, however? That would have caught her attention. Besides, I needed to make a sword that could actually cut through that enchanted skin of hers."

Elva's jaw fell open. "I was a distraction?"

"Well, you were coming here anyway. Might as well use you."

"Why didn't you just tell me that from the beginning?"

Angus gave her an unimpressed look. "Do you really think you would have gone if I told you I had everything handled and I just needed you to stall her?"

No. She likely wouldn't have. Elva wasn't particularly a fan of being the bait dangled in front of enemies. She much preferred to be the person doing the fighting.

She grumbled a quick, "Probably not."

Donnacha burst out laughing and traded his cousin for her. He pulled her tight against him, stealing the breath from her lungs with his hold. "Come on now, faerie. Let's get out of here before the trolls change their mind and decide they'd rather have another fight."

21

Donnacha strode toward his freedom with a feeling of elation fluttering in his breast. How could anyone else understand his emotions right now? The sudden realization that he wasn't cursed anymore and was free from the clutches of the worst sort of faerie.

Elva stalked next to him, her eyes flicking from side to side as she watched the trolls let them leave without complaint. The woman wasn't quite what he expected, he'd admit that.

She'd come all this way for him. Found the troll kingdom, fought the princess, even managed to frighten the Troll Queen before her death. And he had no doubts the Troll Queen had been frightened. Of course, she had.

The beast who had cursed him recognized the kind of faerie who had stood before her. It wasn't the threat that Elva was going to attack her. She hadn't been that kind of nervous. But that this was the future of the faerie realm. A woman who would stand for what she believed in. A woman who could take what she wanted by fire or storm and come out in the end victorious.

Such a creature like Elva would terrify those who followed the old ways. They wouldn't understand the way her blood curdled at the mere thought of chains around her fingers in the form of a wedding ring. They couldn't see the way she affected the world around her without even trying.

Elva was the future of women who were burned by lovers, family, friends. She had endured the flames, and now she walked out of the ashes a new woman. Reborn stronger, deadlier, and infinitely more capable.

He loved her all the more for it.

Angus turned away from the troll kingdom, back toward the home Donnacha desperately wanted to see. the dwarven kingdom whose halls of stone and emeralds called to him.

He wanted to hear the dwarves singing. He wanted to see his family, his friends, all the people who had never given up on him. Even though they hadn't come for him, he had felt their prayers like a wave of cool air every night.

"Bring him home," they had sang to the stars. "Bring him home to our arms."

Could he go that way, though? Elva turned in the opposite direction, magic sparking at her fingertips. She was creating a portal.

Something in him shuddered. He realized, without question that, in that moment, if he let her go now, she would never return. She was afraid of what would happen next. In truth, so was he. What were they now that no curse stood between them?

Were they lovers? Were they fighters who would free others? Or were they infinitely more than that, two halves of a whole who had been searching for each other?

He blew out a breath and looked back at Angus who had paused. They stared at each other for a time, unspoken words flowing between them.

Finally, the dwarf king nodded toward Elva. "I'll see you at home soon."

"It was good to see you."

"And you."

He turned his back on the king and made his way to Elva's side. She'd raised her hands, where glittering gold magic spilled from them.

"You know spells now?" he said quietly, standing behind her so as not to disturb.

"I've always known spells."

"You never used them."

Elva looked at him over her shoulder, not stopping the wave like movement of her fingers. "I couldn't."

"What changed?"

"You."

She looked away from him then, and he was glad for it. His chest had expanded so much in masculine pride he was embarrassed. But hell, she'd just said he was the reason why she could use magic again, and damned if that wasn't better than anything else he'd ever heard in his life.

A bright spot of golden light opened on the ground. He'd never seen a portal that looked like that. She'd created it, though, and that meant he was going to walk through it with her.

Elva tucked her hands behind her back and slowly turned toward him. "I guess this is where we part."

"Why?"

She shook her head. "Why what?"

"Why are we parting?"

"What else would we do?"

Donnacha pointed at the portal behind her. "I'm coming with you."

"No, you aren't. Why would you do that?" She appeared confused, an expression he'd never seen before on her face. "You should go back with your people."

"My place is with you." He stepped forward and lifted a hand to touch her cheek. "I don't know why you crossed the entire Otherworld to get me back, but I do know I don't want to lose that. And you're running, so I'm going to follow you wherever you go."

"I'm not running."

"Yes, you are." He smoothed his thumb over the high peaks of her cheekbones. "But that's okay. I know you're afraid. I am, too. We'll figure this out together. Now tell me, where are you running off to?"

Elva swallowed hard. "The Raven Kingdom."

That place was one of the most dangerous in all of the Otherworld. He'd only heard horror stories coming out of that kingdom, and it wasn't the good kind of horror stories. He swallowed hard in return. "Why are we going there?"

"My sister lives there. I wanted to talk to her, considering I almost just died."

"You didn't almost die."

"But I could have. And that put everything in a little more perspective. I lost her a long time ago and I never tried to find her." Elva shook her head in his grasp. "I don't tell anyone that. I don't know why I'm telling you."

"Because you trust me. What happened to her?"

"We let her be a changeling. Threw her away to the humans, and she wanted me to find her. I didn't. I didn't even try. Instead, I married the Seelie King, ruined my life, and then when she found me years later, I didn't try to keep her with me then either. I've been trying to make up for that ever since."

He knew a thing or two about families who were difficult. His own didn't really want him around, thus how he ended up cursed because he was wandering through the woods outside the mines when he shouldn't have been.

Donnacha nodded. "Okay, let's go talk with her then."

She stared down into his eyes, confusion clouding her own. "That's it?"

"That's it."

"Just…let's go see your sister? No hesitation, no additional thoughts, nothing else to say?"

"Elva, she's your sister. I don't know the woman, so what else could I possibly add to this conversation? I don't know how to change her mind, and I'm certainly not going to tell you the right way to deal with her. I have no doubt if you want to fix this, you will. But we should probably go now or your portal is going to collapse on itself."

Elva slowly nodded. "Yes, let's go then."

"You look like you have more to say."

"I don't know what I want to say to you. You're a confusing man, Donnacha."

He shrugged. "You wouldn't be the first person to say it. Now, come on, let's go to the Raven Kingdom, of all places. Are the soldiers going to attack us immediately?"

"Of course not. We might not get along, but she's still my sister. I have permission to create portals whenever I want."

She made her way toward the portal, and he followed on her heels. He reached out his hand for her to take. She slid her fingers into his the moment before she tugged him into the magic.

A popping sound echoed in his ears as they traveled through the Otherworld at a speed he couldn't even fathom. They stepped from the portal seconds later into the center of a great hall where construction was in full blast.

Donnacha tried to keep his jaw shut as he looked up. Banshee's hovered in the air above them, white gowns floating as if they were underwater as they repaired the stained glass on the ceiling. A dullahan in front of them tossed his head to a dearg-due who stood on a ladder. The vampire woman held the head up high enough for him to look into the rafters where he then shouted, "All good!"

The marble floor beneath their feet was cracked, and he had a few ideas on how to fix that easier than the sluggish dark shadows that slithered over the floor.

Why was the Raven Kingdom filled with such strange creatures? It was uncomfortable to be around them, even though he knew they were technically his brethren, faeries as well.

Elva didn't even flinch or look at the creatures. She stomped toward a woman who stood with bird-like creatures surrounding her. The woman was the mirror image of Elva, strangely enough. But where Elva was light, the other woman was dark. Black hair, pale skin, and eyes exactly the same as Elva.

The sister pointed up at something in the ceiling, unaware that her sister was advancing. One of the bird creatures pointed at Elva the moment before she grabbed her sister's shoulder.

Donnacha winced. Was she going to hit her? Probably not the best way to greet siblings, although he shouldn't intervene.

Instead of striking her, however, Elva tugged the sister into her arms and didn't let go even when the other woman struggled.

Donnacha watched the strange greeting with a smile on his face. She was pretty, this sister. Not in the same way as Elva, who seemed to burn with the fires of the sun. But in the mysterious way the moon gazed down at the earth. Untouchable, glowing with a silver light.

Someone grunted beside him. "I figured they'd get over their own issues eventually."

Donnacha looked beside him and tried not to gape at what was clearly the Raven King. The man was impossibly tall. His dark hair was tied back from his face with a leather thong, dark feathers laced between the strands. It was his eyes that were terrifying, however. One dark human eye, the other a yellow raven eye surrounded by downy feathers.

The Raven King looked back at him. "I'm Bran."

"The man who Elva talks about?" Donnacha carefully didn't say the man she was in love with once, the one she cast aside for the Seelie King and who she still regretted letting go. Although she hadn't said the last part, Donnacha had understood what she was implying.

Bran nodded. “One and the same.”

“And the sister?”

“Aisling. My wife.”

Relief made Donnacha’s vision blur for a moment. The man was married. That was rare in faerie culture and boded well that he wasn’t going to try to steal Elva back. Because this one could. Hell, he might be terrifying, but he was still an impressively handsome man. Even Donnacha could see that.

Bran held out his hand. “I take it you’re her partner now?”

“In a way.” Donnacha shook the offered hand. “Although, probably not in the way you’re thinking.”

A dark, feathered brow lifted. “Ah. Interesting. I didn’t think she was capable of that.”

“Neither did she.”

The hand in his tightened, and Bran tugged him forward until they were far closer than Donnacha was comfortable being.

The Raven King quietly murmured, “If you hurt her, I will break every bone in your body. Slowly and very thoroughly.”

“And if you think she can’t protect herself, then you don’t know her as well as you think.”

Bran released him with a chuckle. “I think I might like you, for all that you are a dwarf.”

“That’s better than most faeries I’ve met.”

Donnacha didn’t particularly like the man standing beside him, but he respected him. The Raven King was far different than most of the royals. He cared for Elva, that was clear, but perhaps in a brotherly way that made it a little easier to swallow.

The women were walking toward them,. He straightened his spine and tried to be a little taller. Everyone else was significantly taller than him, although Elva was at least the shortest in the room.

Why had she let him come, he wondered? After all they’d been through, he considered them friends certainly. But there had also been moments when he'd been convinced they were more than that.

Now, staring at the beautiful faeries standing around him, he wondered why she even bothered letting him into her life. They were all so much...more than him.

Bran crossed his arms over his chest and stared at his wife. "Did you figure it out?"

"Not yet," she replied, "but maybe someday."

"Well, it's a start."

The dark woman turned her eyes to his and narrowed them. "Who are you?"

He didn't have a response for that. He was Donnacha, a dwarf, in a place where he felt very much out of place among faeries who were all infinitely more attractive than him. That was an odd feeling. He didn't know where to go from here.

Opening his mouth, fully aware whatever came out was going to be ridiculous words, he was interrupted by Elva.

"He's mine," she said.

"Yours?" her sister asked with a cough. "What in the world does that mean?"

"I don't really know." Elva looked at him with something new in her eyes, a softness he had only seen during the ball. "I hope you'll stick around for a while, Donnacha, so we might see what this becomes."

The room around them melted away until all he could see was her face. It didn't matter there were dozens of faeries who could hear him, or that her sister and ex-lover stood close enough to touch. He had eyes only for her. "Here?"

She smiled. "No, not in the Raven Kingdom. This isn't home. I don't really have a place where I call home."

"You don't want to live with Scáthach, do you?"

"No."

"Then how about with me?" he asked. "I know it's a larger step, but we don't have to live in the mines with the others. They wouldn't let me back so soon after a curse anyway. We could have a little home. It won't be anything you're used to, of course. No castle nor manor."

"I lived with Scáthach's warriors for the past ten years," she said, stepping closer to him. "I think I'll be fine in a small house."

"A hut really."

"Dirt floors?"

He reached for her, drawing her closer into his arms. "Dirt floors, thatch roof, probably a fireplace that belches smoke back into the room."

"But will you be there?"

"As much as I can be."

Elva leaned down and brushed her lips against his. "Then that's where I want to be."

EPILOGUE

The wheat field spread out around Elva, golden in the sunlight. It was quite possibly the most beautiful field she'd ever seen. She lounged on a blue blanket with the tiniest version of herself.

"Tie this little bit here." She wrapped the tail end of flowers in her hands and watched her daughter mimic the movement.

"Like this?"

"Perfect. Then you loop one more time and you're done."

Her daughter, the blond little sprite who was the spitting image of Elva, held up the flower crown in her hands. "I did it!"

The smile on Elva's face felt as though it might break her cheeks. "Look how beautiful it is!"

It was not, in fact, beautiful. Actually, it was rather droopy, and her daughter had knocked off more than a few petals from the flowers. Annaleise wasn't very careful in her artworks, but it didn't matter. This was still the most beautiful crown Elva had ever seen.

They traded flowers and Elva popped her daughter's creation on her head. "See? Isn't it lovely?"

"You're always lovely, mamaí."

The amount of love she felt for this little thing frightened her sometimes.

Another voice shouted across the field. "Mamaí!"

Elva turned to see her first child, her son, sprinting across the field toward her. He was a dark little thing with hair as black as night. His eyes were hers, though, blue as the sky in the clearest noon.

He raced toward her and launched himself into her arms. Dirt smudged his cheek and the white shirt he wore.

"What did you do today?" she asked, licking her thumb and wiping at the mud. "You're all dirty!"

"Dadaí took me into the mines!"

"I thought we said it was too dangerous for someone your age."

"I'm ten. I can go into the mines now! All the other dwarves are doing it by now."

She didn't have it in her heart to say he took after her more than his father. Though he looked like Donnacha, Iain was going to be as tall as she was. Annaleise, however, was going to be as short as a dwarf and likely have a thick beard like the rest of them.

The father of her children approached them with a broad grin on his face. Time had aged Donnacha as it did all dwarves. The lines around his eyes were deeper and a thin thread of gray had spread from his temple.

He was just as handsome as ever.

Dirt smudged her husband as well, covered him in fact. Elva rolled her eyes and placed her son on the ground. "Take your sister back to the house."

"Mamaí," Iain whined.

"Go on."

He took his younger sister in his arms and scampered toward the small hut with pink roses growing all around it. A curl of smoke lifted into the air, and a goat feasted on grass in the front where she'd tied it to a post.

Donnacha placed a hand on her waist and turned her to him.

Dirty and grinning, he leaned up to plant a kiss firmly to her mouth. “Hello, wife.”

“Hello, husband.”

“Do you know how happy I am with you?”

She grinned. “Well, you only tell me every day.”

“And I will tell you each and every day we are together.” He pulled her closer, pressing another kiss to her lips before pulling back. “I love you, Elva. More than the sun in the sky.”

In that moment and every moment after, she was infinitely happy. After all the struggle, all the times when she had hated the world and herself, Elva had finally found her home.

AFTERWORD

This was a very difficult story for me to write. I'm sure some of my fans and dear friends picked up on the small hints throughout the previous books. Elva's story hits close to home for me.

I almost didn't want to write her story because it felt a bit too much like I was baring my soul, and my editor mentioned that I pulled a few punches that really could have hit home.

However, I felt it was necessary to write this side of the tale. To breathe life into the struggles that a lot of women survive through.

Relationships can be hard. Memories of relationships can be even more difficult, when you wonder if you were the problem all along.

In the end, I hope you know that whatever you decide is right. However you heal, that is the right answer for yourself.

And that no matter what, I'm here to talk. Your healing is more important than anything else.

You are strong.

You are capable.

And you are loved.

ALSO BY EMMA HAMM

The journey began in HEART OF THE FAE, a Beauty and the Beast retelling.

Continued in VEINS OF MAGIC, the second book in the Beauty and the Beast Duology.

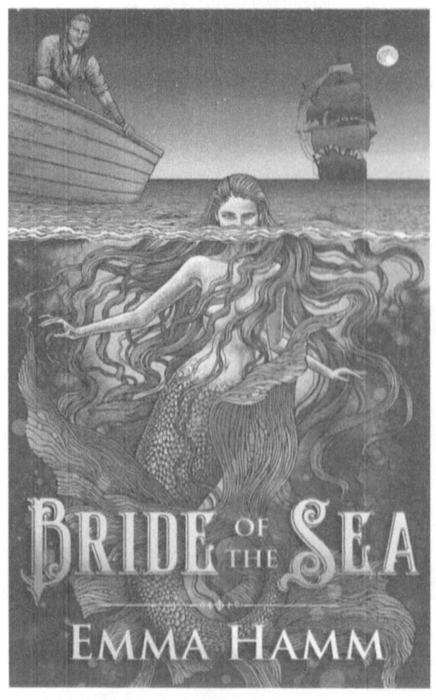

Dove beneath the waves in BRIDE OF THE SEA, an Otherworld Companion Novel and retelling of The Little Mermaid.

We met the Unseelie Prince and Witch in THE FACELESS WOMAN, the first book in the Swan Princess Duology.

We continued their story in The RAVEN'S BALLAD, the second book in the Swan Princess Duology.

ABOUT THE AUTHOR

Emma Hamm grew up in a small town surrounded by trees and animals. She writes strong, confident, powerful women who aren't afraid to grow and make mistakes. Her books will always be a little bit feminist, and are geared towards empowering both men and women to be comfortable in their own skin.